'You're imagir

Rose spoke sharply

'Am I? Well, I'd better apologise, hadn't I?' David's smile was gently mocking and Rose felt resentful. She had an uncomfortable feeling that he knew she was hiding something from him.

'Do you think you could come out of that trance into which the mention of your former fiancé seems to have sent you?' He shook his head slowly. 'I do hope that I won't regret having engaged two people who once were very close.'

Mary Bowring was born in Suffolk, educated in a convent school in Belgium, and joined the WAAF during World War II, when she met her husband. She began to write after the birth of her two children, and published three books about her life as a veterinary surgeon's wife before turning to medical stories.

Recent titles by the same author:

VET WITH A SECRET

VETS AT
CROSS PURPOSES

BY

MARY BOWRING

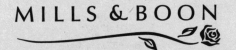

MILLS & BOON

First published in Great Britain 2000
Harlequin Mills & Boon Limited,
Eton House, 18-24 Paradise Road, Richmond, Surrey TW9 1SR

© Mary Bowring 2000

ISBN 0 263 81915 9

Set in Times Roman 10½ on 12¼ pt.
03-0001-47181

Printed and bound in Spain
by Litografía Rosés S.A., Barcelona

CHAPTER ONE

ROSE DEAKIN, MRCVS, stared at her fiancé in consternation. 'But it's a lovely job,' she protested, 'in charge of the small animal side of Mr Langley's practice. It was having had two years' practice that clinched it. He didn't want a newly qualified vet—he already has one who apparently needs an experienced senior to whom she can refer for advice if necessary.'

Pete Harlow shook his head impatiently. 'That's all beside the point. You can't take the job.'

'You're crazy!' Rose's blue eyes flashed. 'I've already accepted. I move into the cottage in a month and start work on the Monday. Why on earth are you so against it?'

He hesitated, gave a quick glance round the crowded country pub, picked up his glass, drained it and said softly, 'We can't talk here. Come round to my house—no, better not. We'll talk in my car.'

'Good grief!' Rose showed her irritation by staying seated. 'Tell me here. All this secrecy is absurd.'

He stood, frowning down at her. 'Listen—you don't know how important this is to me. Let me explain in the car.'

'Oh, all right.' She got up reluctantly. 'But nothing is going to make me change my mind.' She sighed as they went outside. 'I thought you would

5

have been thrilled to have me working in the same practice—you doing the large animals and me working in the surgery. When I saw that advertisement in the *Veterinary Record* it seemed like an answer to our problem.'

'You should have asked me before you applied,' he said as he held the passenger door open.

As she seated herself, she said, 'I wanted to surprise you. Now I am the one who is surprised. Surprised and angry.'

As they wended their way through the Sussex village towards the downs, Rose's mind was confused. Her fiancé's reception of what she had thought was good news was so unexpected that she was stunned. Apprehensive, too, because it was evident that they were heading for a quarrel. Engaged for only six months, she had already been starting to wonder whether she had committed herself too soon.

Still suffering from the trauma of her twin brother's death in a car accident, she had found comfort in Pete's warm sympathy. Gradually the casual friendship had developed until at last it had seemed inevitable that they should get engaged. Originally working together in a large practice in the Midlands where there were several partners, it was obvious that they should seek employment elsewhere.

To Pete it was imperative that in order to advance in his career he should get a partnership, but for Rose it was enough to feel happy and fulfilled in her work. Compassionate and tender in her dealings with animals, she was very accurate in diagnoses and an extremely skilful surgeon. Suddenly Pete's voice broke into her thoughts.

'I know it was a bit of a shock to you when I left to take up my new job with Mr Langley, but you soon agreed that it was too good to miss—the promise of a partnership in six months if mutually suited.

'We also agreed that you should get an assistant's job as near to me as possible. Well, there are lots of veterinary practices in Sussex, so why on earth you had to go and get yourself taken on by Mr Langley is beyond me.' He shook his head and added bitterly, 'You've ruined my chance of a partnership— I suppose you know that.'

'That's ridiculous. Why on earth do you say that?'

'You'll understand soon enough,' he snapped, and fell silent as he turned the car into the long, winding road across the downs. Eventually he pulled up, facing the sea. Getting out, he joined Rose and they stood silently, looking at the magnificent view spread out before them. The incoming tide was gradually enveloping the seaweed-covered rocks and an oil tanker was slowly chugging along in the blue distance, looking far more romantic than it really was.

That, thought Rose, is what my engagement is like—romantic as seen from a distance, but in reality a rather dull affair. Watching the seagulls soaring above and below them, she waited for Pete to break the silence, which he seemed reluctant to do. At last he flung himself down on the grass.

Patting the springy turf he said, 'It's quite dry.'

She nodded and sat down beside him, folding her

arms round her knees and drawing in long breaths of salty air. Then her momentary pleasure in her surroundings faded as Pete began to talk.

'When Mr Langley agreed to take me on he asked me something that should have put me on my guard, but at the time it didn't register. It was just before we got engaged and I wasn't even sure that you would say yes, so when he asked me if I was married, engaged or even in a steady relationship, I said no. That seemed to please him. He went on to tell me that he had nothing against any of these things so long as I wasn't tied up with a woman vet.'

He paused as Rose gasped in indignation. Then he went on, 'Yes, it startled me a bit, so I asked why. He just shrugged and said it had been his experience that in view of the long, irregular hours of veterinary work a great deal of strain was put on marriages and relationships. This naturally affected their work and, if they worked in the same practice it meant big trouble.'

He paused. 'So the six months he offered me was tied up with his bigoted views.'

Rose looked thoughtful. 'I wouldn't say he is bigoted. As a matter of fact, I found him, well, rather nice. He told me to call him David. It's all first names in the practice apparently.'

Pete shrugged impatiently. 'Well, I always think of him as Mr Langley—to tell the truth I'm rather in awe of him. He is very reserved—keeps his distance. Actually, I don't like him very much.'

'Well, that's not a very good outlook for the future, then.' Rose looked troubled but Pete gave a short laugh.

'I don't show how I feel. I do my best to butter him up. I want that partnership badly. No need to look so disapproving, Rose.'

She opened her mouth to remonstrate but he said suddenly, 'Did he ask you if you were engaged or anything?'

'No. The question never came up. Perhaps it was because when he showed me the cottage he apologised for it being so small, but I said it was ideal for me.'

'But your engagement ring—didn't he see that?' Then, glancing down at Rose's left hand, he exclaimed, 'Good Lord! You haven't got it on. Where is it?'

She shrugged. 'If you remember, it was just a bit too big for my finger. I shan't get it back till next week.'

Pete's eyes brightened. 'That's a bit of luck. He need never know about our engagement.'

Rose stared, shocked at his suggestion. 'He's bound to find out eventually because whatever you say I'm going to take this job. He may change his mind about married vets working together if I can prove myself in the surgery.'

'But…but…' Pete looked aghast. 'You can't— don't you understand? However good you are, it would still mean that I wouldn't get the partnership. I've told you, he won't have a married couple working in his practice.' He looked at her pleadingly. 'Oh, Rose, tell him you've changed your mind and say you've got another job—it doesn't matter. Wait until I've got the partnership all signed and legally binding.'

He rose to his feet and walked up and down, deep in thought. Then he came back and looked at her earnestly. 'Listen, if you insist on taking this job we'll have to pretend we don't even know each other. Don't wear your ring, don't tell the rest of the staff—there are only two nurses and the other vet, Susan. We'll just keep our engagement completely quiet. Look, we must work this out carefully.'

Rose looked at him coldly. 'I'm no good at deception and I'm not a liar. You're asking me to cheat and pretend.' She paused. 'There's only one way to solve this problem.'

He looked uneasy. 'What's that, then?'

She drew a long breath, hesitated for a moment then said, 'Break off our engagement.'

He looked stunned then he said uneasily, 'You're joking, of course. You can't mean—'

'But I do mean it. In fact, I think that quite apart from this job I've taken I would rather like to be free again—like to have some time to reconsider our engagement. We did rather drift into it, didn't we?'

He flushed angrily. 'Well, that was your fault. I wanted you to move in with me but you wouldn't. This waiting until we're married is bound to put a strain on any engagement.'

He paused and then, as they stayed silent, he added slowly, 'I tell you what, if I agree to breaking our engagement and we work together in the same practice we could have the occasional night to-

gether—nobody need know—then when I become a
partner we could become officially engaged and
Langley wouldn't be able to do anything about it.'

He paused and gave a triumphant laugh. 'That's
it. That's the answer to the problem.'

Rose looked at him despairingly. This was the
man she had thought would make the ideal husband.
Instead, he was devious, unscrupulous and determined to get his own way by whatever means.

He was watching her expression and at last he
said, 'Don't look so disapproving, Rose. It's a great
idea—that way we can have the best of both worlds.
It would be amusing to fool everyone—be lovers on
the quiet and quite indifferent to each other in public.'

'Amusing to you perhaps, but hateful to me.' She
looked at him steadily. 'No, Pete, it's all off, and if
David Langley asks any awkward questions I shall
tell him the truth. That I was once engaged to you
but I've broken it off.'

She got to her feet and glanced at her watch. 'I've
got to go. I don't want to be late back.' She hesitated
then said resolutely, 'I'll send my engagement ring
back to you.'

He caught up with her as she began to walk back.
'Rose, you can't do this to me. All our plans for the
future thrown away just because you—'

'Because I want to work here. You know as well
as I do that we both want to get away from John
Marston's practice—it's too far, too big and too im-
personal—and it's lovely here on the South Coast.'
She paused. 'David Langley is very nice. I find it

difficult to believe that he has a chip on his shoulder.'

'Oh, I suppose Langley's not too bad. I've been here two months now and I'm pretty sure he'll offer me the partnership when the six months' trial period is up. So, Rose...' He stopped and put his arm around her. 'As soon as I get it I'll ask you again and to hell with Langley's daft ideas.' He turned her towards him. 'One kiss and, please, promise that you will still consider that we are engaged.'

She let him kiss her but in her heart she knew that it was all over between them. Looking up at him she said quietly, 'I can't make that promise, Pete. I realise now that all I feel for you is friendship and I'm sure that eventually you'll be glad to have your freedom, as glad as I am.'

Releasing her quickly, he said furiously, 'Maybe I will. I never realised before that you could be so hard and self-seeking.' He paused and went on bitterly, 'I'm not even going to wish you luck when you take up work here. In fact, I hope you won't find it as pleasant as you expect.'

He gave a short laugh. 'What's more, as soon as I'm a partner I promise I'll do my best to make you wish you'd never played this dirty trick on me.'

She stifled a gasp and merely shrugged at his angry threat. But, driving back to the Midlands, she found it difficult to shake off the chill that enveloped her. Heavy traffic made it impossible for her to sort out her feelings until at last she reached her destination. Locking up her car, she let herself into her flat and sank into a chair with a sigh of relief.

Staring into space, she thought that she ought to prepare some kind of a meal, but with no appetite she eventually settled for a sandwich and coffee. She sat, brooding over the day's events and marvelling at the way things had turned out. She had set out that morning visualising the pleasure it would give Pete to hear that she was going to join him in David Langley's practice, only to return utterly disillu-sioned.

Disillusioned, but free from an engagement that, although she had tried to suppress the doubts that had been in her subconscious mind for some time, would have led to disaster. Now the only doubt that troubled her was whether she ought to abandon the idea of working in the same practice as Pete. But that, she told herself, would be admitting defeat and losing a job that she longed to take. As described by David Langley, it was very attractive with a good salary and a step up from her present position.

David himself had been very straightforward and was the kind of dedicated vet she'd always admired. A picture of him rose in her mind's eye and she dwelt on it thoughtfully. A tall man with a face that was strong yet sensitive. Dark brown hair that fell occasionally over grey eyes that, though when in repose seemed to hold a hint of sadness, lit up with laughter when called for.

His voice was deep and reassuring, and altogether it seemed extraordinary that such a pleasant man could hold such strange views with regard to his staff. In any case it didn't matter now. She and Pete were no longer engaged and there was nothing to hide. She finished her sandwich and glanced at her watch. Tomorrow she must hand in her resignation.

During the month that followed Rose worked with her usual dedication. Then, after spending a few days with her parents, she set off for Westmouth. For the first part of her journey her feelings were mixed. The life she was leaving behind had been one of easy acceptance of work in a large practice—pleasant enough with her colleagues, but often unsatisfactory when it came to following up her patients' progress. Often she had been irritated when her verdicts had been overruled and treatment changed during her absence.

Then there had been Pete and the way in which it had been accepted by everyone that they were a couple and would eventually become engaged. She shook her head slowly as she sped along the motorway. What a mistake she had made there. It was only when he had been so angry that she had seen him in his true colours. Well, that was over and she was now on the verge of a new life. Her spirits rose.

On arrival at her destination she found to her pleasure that David Langley was waiting to accompany her to her cottage. After handing her the keys, he said, 'You've had quite a long drive—have you had any lunch?'

She shook her head. 'I stopped for a coffee but I never have much in the middle of the day anyway. Once I've arranged my things I'll make a sandwich. There is plenty here—it was kind of you to have the fridge so well stocked.'

'I have a better idea. Come and have a pub lunch

with me. It would be a good opportunity for me to put you in the picture with regard to the practice.'

She had not expected such a courteous welcome and when she was seated opposite him in the pleasant little pub he had chosen she said as much.

He smiled. 'Well, of course. You are going to be a very important member of the practice, in full control of the small animal side, which is expanding all the time.' He paused. 'I bought this practice three years ago from old Mr Barton and it was a bit run down at the time. He worked single-handed, with some help from his wife. Then she left him and after that he lost interest and his clients faded away. So I've had quite a job, building it up almost from scratch.'

He shrugged. 'That sounds a bit boastful but it wasn't all that difficult because I was able to borrow from a family trust and last year my father died, leaving me financially secure. I hope I'm not embarrassing you with such personal details but I don't think there should be any secrets between colleagues.'

Suddenly Rose felt a pang of alarm and as he went on she waited apprehensively for what inevitably had to come. After speaking appreciatively about Susan, the other vet, and the two veterinary nurses, Wendy and Penny, he paused and added, 'Then there is Pete—a prospective partner who is subject to the usual six-month trial period. He came here two months ago from—' He stopped and Rose's heart seemed to stop too as his eyes widened.

'Why, of course, I meant to ask you at our interview if you knew him, seeing that you came from the same practice, but I forgot.' He laughed. 'I was distracted by—well, you are a bit distracting to the average male, aren't you?'

His mouth twitched at the corner and her colour rose as he continued, 'Anyway, as you both come from the same practice you must already know him.' He paused again. 'When I told Pete you were coming we were interrupted by an emergency and I don't think he had the opportunity of answering.'

It was here—the question she had been dreading—but, taking a deep breath to calm herself, Rose shrugged indifferently. 'Oh, yes. We were friends. He qualified two years before I did.'

'I see.' David's steady gaze almost unnerved her, especially in view of his remark about no secrets between colleagues. Then suddenly he said, '*Were* friends—why the past tense?'

She could feel the blood draining from her face. All the explanations she had prepared vanished and she knew she could hide nothing from those keen grey eyes, gazing at her so steadily. She swallowed hard. 'We were engaged.'

'Ah!' he nodded slowly. 'Once—all over now?'

'Yes. All over now.'

There was a long silence, which seemed to Rose to go on for ever, then he asked her quietly, 'So why did you apply for this job when you must have known that Pete was already here?'

'We were still engaged and I thought it would be nice to work in the same practice. Then we broke

up and I didn't see why I should give up this job
that I had applied for.'

She saw his eyes grow cold and added, 'Pete
means nothing to me now so my work here won't
suffer.'

'How does Pete feel about it?'

'Well, he doesn't like it. In fact, he tried to persuade me to give up the idea of taking this job.'

He nodded. 'I can see his point. In fact, I should
feel the same. You're very beautiful. Gorgeous dark
hair. You were well named—Rose.'

Suddenly Rose felt angry. She had answered his
questions and not given away Pete's real character.
Now it seemed she was being put in the wrong. She
said sharply, 'Well, in view of your obvious disap-
proval, do you want me to leave? If so...' she
shrugged '...I'll go right now. I shan't hold you to
our contract. As a matter of fact, I don't think it's
anything to do with you.'

'Oh, dear!' Suddenly he laughed. 'Temper!
Temper! You're right, of course. I shouldn't have
put you through such an interrogation. All the same,
my sympathies are with Pete. Poor chap! I just hope
your presence won't affect his work.'

'Of course it won't. Don't—don't imagine he's
broken hearted or anything. We both realize we
made a mistake, that's all.'

'I see.' David nodded, then he added thoughtfully,
'You know that Pete is on a six-month trial for a
partnership? That is, if we are mutually suited.' He
paused as she nodded then went on, 'What you may
not know is that I have an objection—some might

call it a bee in my bonnet—to having a married couple, both vets, working in the same practice.'

He paused. 'Well, my practice anyway.' He was looking at Rose so searchingly that her heart seemed to miss a beat and her mouth went dry with apprehension.

There was only one answer she could give and she said, 'Yes. Pete told me.'

'Ah!' Now there was an angry glint in his eyes. 'So that was why you both decided to become, well, disengaged, was it? No, wait—' He saw her furious reaction but continued relentlessly, 'Then once Pete had got his partnership you could then fall in love with each other again and get married, thus overcoming my personal dislike of such a situation. Who thought that one up? You or Pete?'

Remembering that this was exactly what Pete had suggested, and knowing she could not betray him, Rose said sharply, 'That's a beastly idea! If you think I'm capable of such deceit then it is obvious that I can't work for you.' She made to get up but he reached out and put his hand on her shoulder, pressing her down.

'Hold it! Hold it! No need to get so upset. I believe you and apologise abjectly for misjudging you. Now, let me tell you my future plans for the practice. I need two partners—one male and one female. I am going to start up a branch practice—small animals mostly—and once you have helped Susan to stand on her own feet you could, if you wished, take over the new practice as a partner and be in full charge.'

He paused and smiled. 'Conditional, of course, on our mutual compatibility.'

Rose stared at him speechlessly. She opened her mouth but no words came and he laughed at her confusion.

'No need to commit yourself. It's all in the future, but I'd like you to bear it in mind. Now, please forgive me for doubting your integrity.'

Still dazed, Rose managed a tremulous smile and tried to concentrate as he went on to discuss the way he ran his practice and the various difficulties that sometimes occurred.

At last, with a quick glance at his watch, he said, 'I expect you'd like to get back to the cottage. If there is anything you need, just let me know—otherwise, I'll see you on Monday morning.'

For the rest of the day Rose spent her time arranging things to her liking. The cottage was indeed small but compact, with a good-sized living room, small kitchen and two bedrooms—one overlooking the front, which she chose for herself, and a tiny one at the back. It stood alone about a mile from the surgery and it suited Rose down to the ground. Eventually she went to bed, promising herself that the next day she would drive round the area so as to be able to find her way to the nearest town and memorise the names of the villages scattered about.

Next morning, sitting over breakfast coffee, she mulled over David's proposition. A partnership for her, involving the running of a future branch practice—it was a fabulous offer. If it were not for Pete she would jump at the chance. She sighed. Best not take it too seriously.

The thought of Pete made her resolve to spend this Sunday out all day, in case he should take it into his head to visit her. He must be kept at a distance, otherwise it might lead to unpleasant complications. Studying a map of the district, which she found on a side table, she marked out a route which covered what she considered to be the extent of the practice.

Just as she was about to set out there was a ring at the front door. Her heart sank as she saw Pete standing outside. She opened the door, but said quickly, 'I'm just going out. In any case, I don't think you should be here. I thought we agreed to be just casual friends, meeting only during working hours.'

His smile faded. 'That's ridiculous. It's only natural that, having heard you are here, I should look you up.' He pushed past her into the sitting room and stood, waiting for her to shut the door.

As she turned towards him he said, 'I've got a bone to pick with you. You've put me in a very difficult position. I saw David yesterday evening and he told me you had said that we were once engaged. He even commiserated with me, saying that you were such a lovely girl and that I must be feeling sore. Of course I denied this and said we had broken up by mutual consent and were just friends.'

He paused, and Rose breathed a sigh of relief and said, 'Well, that's true, isn't it? That's what I told him.'

'You needn't have mentioned our engagement at all,' he said angrily. 'Now he'll be watching us all the time to see if we are carrying on secretly.'

'What do you mean by "carrying on"?' she asked indignantly. 'You know very well that it's all over between us. There will be no secret meetings.' She went across to the window then turned. 'What's more, I'd be glad if you didn't call here any more. Your car is quite distinctive and before we know it people will be gossiping.'

'You really mean it, then?' Suddenly he looked so sad that she felt a small pang of pity for him.

'I was hoping that sometimes you would spend the night with me for old times' sake.'

Pity disappeared immediately, to be replaced by indignant scorn. 'Look, Pete, I wouldn't move in with you even when we were engaged so why on earth should I risk both our jobs here by doing such a stupid thing?'

'I suppose you're right.' He shrugged despondently.

'Especially in my case. After all, there's more at stake for me than there is for you.'

She hesitated for a moment. No, she wouldn't tell him of David's offer of a partnership for her as well. Let sleeping dogs lie. It might never come off. She held the door open but he said sulkily, 'Don't I even get a cup of coffee?'

'No,' she said firmly, 'and the sooner you're gone the better. I don't like seeing your car outside.'

He slammed his way out and she was left with an uneasy feeling as she watched him drive away. Was he going to make things difficult? Surely not, because it would be against his own interests and with Pete that was always the main consideration. Suddenly she sighed. Perhaps it would have been better if she had not taken this job. For a few moments she pondered the situation then she shrugged off her doubts.

If things got too tangled she could always leave, though it would be with regret because there was something about David Langley that attracted her. It was his dislike of deceit in any shape or form and his immediate apology when he felt he had misjudged her. She could only hope that Pete would not make trouble for her in revenge for having been so thoroughly rejected.

CHAPTER TWO

ON MONDAY Rose went into the surgery half an hour early and was pleased to see that Susan, her veterinary colleague, was already there. They had been introduced when Rose had been formally accepted for the position, but the meeting had been cut short by an emergency and Rose had not been able to gain much idea of what it was going to be like, working together.

Half an hour was quite sufficient for them to sum each other up and Rose was delighted to find that, far from being resentful, Susan welcomed her with obvious relief. She was a tall, pretty girl with fair hair, cut short, and she had a cheerful, open manner. Seemingly confident, she confessed to an inward apprehension when confronted by a patient with puzzling symptoms or with a difficult client.

She laughed. 'Now I'll be able to refer them to you. Apart from that, we have such busy surgeries that it's almost too much for just one vet.' She paused. 'Our nurses will be in soon. They really are marvellous girls. The elder—Wendy—is very practical and tactful with difficult clients, and Penny keeps us all looking on the bright side when things get a bit traumatic.'

She was silent for a moment then added thoughtfully, 'As for David, well...' She shrugged. 'We all think he is marvellous. Kind, understanding and absolutely straight in his dealings. He tells us quite openly of any difficulties occurring in the practice. Then there's Pete—he's being considered for a partnership. He's very nice, too.'

She smiled. 'The word has gone round that you two know each other. Is that so?'

'Oh, yes,' Rose said easily. 'We've known each other for years. Same town, same university, only he was two years ahead of me. We both worked in the local veterinary practice for a while.'

'Goodness! How strange—you seem to have followed in his footsteps all the time,' Susan exclaimed, then looked puzzled. 'Whose idea was it that you should come here?'

'Mine,' Rose said briefly. 'I saw the position advertised in the *Veterinary Record* and the fact that Pete was here really had nothing to do with it.' She stopped at the obvious disbelief in Susan's face and hated herself for the necessary lie.

She added hastily, 'When I told Pete he wasn't best pleased, but...' she shrugged and laughed '...it does look as though I'm following him everywhere, doesn't it? But I don't see that it matters.'

Even to her own ears her explanation sounded feeble, but she knew this was something she must get used to. To her great relief Susan evidently considered the subject closed and began to explain the surgery layout.

'David has had it all arranged so that we two can work independently. Two consulting rooms, two operating theatres, and so on. Of course, we share certain things, like the x-ray equipment. Dispensary and the office can be used by all four vets.' She paused. 'By the way, David says we must get another VN. He's already interviewed a few. I expect we'll hear soon which one he has chosen.'

She stopped as the door opened. 'Ah, here they are—Wendy and Penny. They're unusually early— I expect it's in order to meet you before surgery begins.'

Rose took to them immediately. Wendy was tall and fair-haired with an open smiling face, and Penny was of medium height with a mane of golden-red hair, tied back now for work but which when loose would be like a brilliant cloud of fire. They only had a quarter of an hour together but it was enough for Rose to realise that she was going to enjoy the company of these friendly, helpful girls.

Their main preoccupation at the moment was the prospect of a new veterinary nurse, and Penny said she was keeping her fingers crossed in the hope that David would choose a friend of hers.

'I recommended her,' she said, 'but David said he would judge each applicant on her capabilities and personality.' She shrugged ruefully. 'Typical of him, of course. Never allows himself to be swayed by other people when it comes to his work.' She sighed. 'I think he is marvellous.'

Wendy laughed. 'Well, we all do but we don't drool over him like you.'

'I don't drool,' Penny said indignantly. 'I just think—' She stopped at the sound of clients arriving in the waiting room and reached for her green surgery overall. 'Ah, well. Another hectic day.'

It certainly was a busy surgery and Rose soon realised that Susan had been doing more than one person's work. There seemed to be a lot of new clients. From what Susan told her, this was always the case in late spring and all through the summer.

'Visitors,' she said. 'People staying in the large hotels and boarding houses where dogs are allowed. Mostly ailments due to holiday conditions—skin irritations caused by rolling in the sand after having been in the sea, stomach upsets, and so on, and, of course, in a heat wave...' She shrugged. 'I sometimes think it would be better if people put their pets into good kennels or catteries, instead of subjecting them to new routines in strange environments.'

But Rose's first patient did not come into that category. A young man was ushered in, followed by Susan who drew Rose aside. 'Here's where I need help. I know very little about ferrets.'

Rose laughed, then a shadow passed over her face momentarily. Recovering, she said, 'My brother used to keep them so...' She looked at the young man and smiled as he came forward with the creamy-coloured ferret curled round his arm.

Holding it out for inspection, he said, 'This is Jake and I can't understand why his coat is so poor and he doesn't seem to grow. This is the first time I've kept a ferret but I've had him injected for all the usual things. He's six months old, but from what I've read he should be about a foot long when he's

fully grown and it doesn't seem to me that he's going to make it.'

Rose handled the pretty creature carefully, putting
him on the table and examining him thoroughly. At
last she looked up. 'What do you feed him on?'

The youth looked surprised. 'Well, I was told that
a diet of bread and milk, along with cat food, was
the best way to feed him, so that's what he's been
having.'

Rose frowned. 'I don't know who gave you that
advice but it's wrong. Unfortunately, a lot of people
do feed ferrets that way, with the result you see
here—hunched back, poor bone structure and a dull
coat that tells of mistaken diet.' She paused.

'They have a shorter digestive tract than cats and
dogs and their natural diet consists of whole small
rodents and the occasional bird. They are capable of
chewing and eating all parts of the carcass, including
bone. Is Jake going to be used for working?
Ferreting, I mean, or is he just a pet?'

'He's a pet. Been brought up like a cat. He's
house-trained, believe it or not. Uses a litter tray and
I take him out walking on a harness. He's affectionate, too, like a cat.'

Rose nodded. 'Yes. They do give a cat-like af-
fection but, as I said, their digestive systems are totally different. They have a rapid growth rate so they
need a good quality balanced diet. Now, in my opinion, this little fellow will not have a long life if you
don't change his food.'

She smiled reassuringly at the young man's dis-
consolate look. 'Don't worry. The problem is easily

resolved. There is a special food for ferrets which is cheap and good. I don't think we have it here but I'll tell you where you can get it and I'm sure Jake will take to it well as it's very palatable.'

The problem solved, and armed with the necessary information, Jake's owner went away happy, with the ferret once more entwined round his arm.

'Well…' Susan drew a long breath. 'They say you learn something new every day—I'm certainly a lot wiser than I was.' She glanced at her watch. 'Surgery's over and the waiting room is empty so let's have coffee.' She looked behind her. 'Yes, Penny has put the kettle on. Time for a break.' She paused. 'Luckily I haven't any ops this morning. What about you?'

Rose shook her head. 'Nothing immediate, but two feline spays to be done tomorrow. This practice certainly needed another small animal vet—how on earth did you manage on your own?'

Susan shrugged. 'Well, sometimes I had to call for help and then either David or Pete would arrange their calls so as to be able to put in an hour with me. The truth is that the practice has grown since David took it over, and one of the reasons for that is that Mr Trent over at Marsden has semi-retired. He now only does inoculations, boosters and suchlike, and recommends his regular clients to come here.

'I suppose when he gives up entirely David will either have to buy his practice or allow a rival to set up there. Knowing David, I expect he'll take it over and use it as a branch practice.'

Rose nodded but kept to herself that David had suggested she herself might be given charge of a future branch. Discretion, she felt, was necessary in this case.

The immediate future was enough to worry about for as Penny began assembling mugs for coffee she said, 'I expect David and Pete will be in soon.' She laughed. 'It's wonderful how they arrange their calls so as to turn up here in time for coffee.'

True to her prophesy, the outer door opened and David entered just as Penny was filling the mugs.

Seating himself next to Rose, he asked smilingly, 'How did your first surgery go?'

'It was quite busy but mostly routine cases—quite a few of the clients were holiday visitors, as Susan had warned me.'

Susan turned to David. 'I was very glad to have Rose to advise me when a ferret turned up.' She laughed ruefully. 'I would probably have prescribed something or other but Rose has had personal experience of ferrets and now I'm a whole lot wiser.'

'Personal experience?' David looked surprised. 'You mean to say that you kept them yourself?' He smiled at Rose. 'Not usual for a woman—no, I'm not being sexist.' He laughed. 'It's a fact.'

She nodded easily. 'True. Actually, the ferrets belonged to my brother so I was force-fed the information from an early age.' She stopped as the door opened again to admit Pete, and her heart jumped uneasily. As he came forward she was aware that David was watching her closely.

Rose took her cue from Pete who said easily, 'Hi,

Rose. So you've arrived. Bit of a change from the Midlands, isn't it?' He turned to David. 'I must say I like the country round here. Lovely air, too. Fills you full of energy.'

After that the atmosphere became relaxed and Rose felt that another hurdle had been overcome. Not that there had been any obvious tension. It was only, Rose told herself, that she had been apprehensive about Pete's possible behaviour at this their first meeting in the presence of all the members of the practice.

Once more the conversation turned back to the ferret and Pete laughed. 'I remember how Rose's brother used to drag everyone to see his prize specimens. Actually, he was very knowledgeable about them, wasn't he, Rose?'

She nodded, not too pleased at his display of close friendship with her and her family. She was about to change the subject when David asked casually, 'What does your brother do? Is he a vet as well?'

Rose swallowed painfully. 'No.' She paused. 'He was killed in a car accident two years ago. He was my twin.'

'Oh, how awful!' Susan's quick sympathy brought tears to Rose's eyes, and it was all she could do to stop them from falling. She picked up her coffee and drank deeply. Putting the mug down, she met David's gaze and saw such kindness in his expression that once more her eyes burned with unshed tears. To her great relief the ringing of the telephone put an end to all emotion and David got to his feet.

'I'll take it,' he said, and as he listened he

frowned. After a few questions he put the receiver down and turned to Rose. 'A nasty incident out at Neston—a village four miles from here. A dog fight. One is badly bitten and the other has run off.' Rose got up. 'I think I'd better take you—it's a difficult place to get at.'

He turned to Susan. 'We'll most likely bring the dog back here and either you or Rose can deal with him.'

She nodded. 'I'll have everything ready—possible anaesthesia, blood transfusion and so on.'

David picked up Rose's case and handed it to her. 'Better take this as well in case we need extra drugs.'

Before she could protest Rose found herself outside, but as David opened the passenger door she said resentfully, 'I do know where Neston is—I explored the countryside yesterday. There really isn't any need for you to côme, you know.' She turned towards her own car but he stood in her way.

'No.' He shook his head firmly. 'That's not the only reason for me to accompany you. I know these people and they're quite unpleasant, believe me. Come on, get in.'

'So you think I may need protection?' The scorn in her voice made him frown.

He said grimly, 'Look at it that way if you like.' Going round the car, he opened his door and seated himself at the wheel. Rose shrugged and got in beside him. As though they had had no disagreement he began to talk easily.

'Last time I was called out there it was also a dog

fight so I'm beginning to wonder what's going on behind the scenes. There are several outhouses behind the house and I've heard dogs barking. When I asked them how many dogs they had they were very evasive—said they were looking after a friend's dogs while he was on holiday. It all looks a bit fishy to me. What do you think?'

Rose was startled. 'You mean that perhaps they're organising dog fights? What kind of dogs are they?'

'Well, the one I saw was a cross pit bull terrier— but, of course, if they are treated badly they can become killers. We'll see if this one we've been called out to is the same breed—maybe even the same dog. As for the one they say ran off—well, who knows? It may well be dead.'

He frowned. 'It's very difficult for vets nowadays. There's the duty of confidentiality—we're bound by that unless we have absolute proof that the law is being broken. Anyway, we'll have to keep our eyes open.'

He pointed ahead some minutes later. 'See that isolated place over there? That's the house. There's a huge barn behind. I wonder…' He said no more and Rose felt apprehensive as they drove into the yard in front of the shabby house.

When two burly, sullen men approached them as they got out of the car she felt even more nervous but, used to disguising her feelings, she gave them a friendly smile which was not returned. Instead, they stared hard.

Turning to David, the one with red hair asked curtly, 'Why are there two of you?'

Once the explanation had been given the men took them into the house where, in the kitchen, they saw the patient lying in a corner on a pile of sacks. Given the task of examining the dog, Rose asked David to hold the bull terrier still, which he did expertly. It was no easy task because the dog was very aggressive in spite of the restraining muzzle. Carefully unwinding the blood-soaked bandage tied loosely across his chest, Rose gasped at the wound.

It was a deep gash about four inches wide, which caused her to look up searchingly at the two men. Her unspoken question forced one of them to growl something about it having been a fight almost to the death.

'The two of them—this one and his attacker— have always hated each other. They're kept apart but somehow…' he shrugged indifferently '…someone must have left a gate open.'

Continuing her examination, Rose drew David's attention to various other bites, and the dog gradually grew more docile under her gentle handling and soothing voice. At last with a quick glance at David, who nodded back, she said, 'Well, I'll give him an injection now for shock and pain relief.'

As David handed her the filled syringes the red-haired man said unpleasantly, 'Well don't overdo the treatment. All he really needs are some stitches here and there. He's a tough dog—he'll soon be OK.'

Rose was about to burst out indignantly but David said quickly, 'I agree. He's a strong dog. What about the other one? Is he the same breed?'

There was a moment's silence then the first man, who had hitherto been silent, said, 'He was a terrier too. They're very popular, especially up north.'

David nodded. 'You said it's run off. Was it also injured?'

The two men glanced at each other, then the red-haired man shrugged. 'Probably not all that badly. He'll turn up eventually.'

'Well, if he needs attention bring him along to us. Don't let him run around with an open wound. That way infection will set in.' He paused. 'Now, will you help me get this one into my car? What's his name, by the way?'

'Satan—and you'll need to keep that muzzle on when you are treating him.'

David nodded. 'Don't worry. We'll cope in spite of his name.' He laughed easily. 'Do you give all your dogs such, well, fierce names? Doesn't that put prospective buyers off?'

'The people we deal with like strong names.' The red-haired man grinned but the other man frowned, obviously disliking being questioned. He slammed the car door shut as Rose got in.

As David turned the ignition key he stood back and said, 'Remember. Don't do anything unnecessary. We don't want a bloody great bill.'

As they drove away David said, 'I'll bet the other dog is a pit bull, and if it's not dead it's tucked away somewhere in the outhouse. Did you notice how when I asked if it was like this one he was rather evasive?' He shook his head thoughtfully. 'Not much we can do about it, I'm afraid.'

Rose said, 'This business of confidentiality—does it mean we can't pass on our suspicions to the police so that they can look into it?'

'No. That's the difficulty. A lot of people want the College to allow vets to breach the confidentiality code in these and other cases, but if that were allowed the rules would virtually cease to exist. And, of course, clients would be hesitant to seek professional advice if it might involve the risk of their affairs being discussed and made known to the police or the RSPCA.

'If even one owner was reported as being under suspicion of participating in organised dog fighting, the word would quickly spread on the grapevine. From then on injured dogs would either go untreated or be treated by lay persons.'

He paused then added slowly, 'Mind you, if someone else tells the police and a prosecution is brought, the vet is free to tell all he knows. But that's very different from the vet being the informer himself. As for this fellow we've got in the back, he is probably one of a few cross-breeds kept as a cover while the pit bulls are hidden away.' He sighed. 'It's all rather difficult, isn't it?'

Rose nodded. 'I suppose the same rules apply to dogs used in the digging out of badgers. How can people be so cruel?'

'I can't answer that,' he said grimly. 'All I know is that in our profession it's not all sweetness and light. There are so many forms of cruelty. Sometimes cold, callous neglect and on the other hand the terrible sentimentality that won't allow an animal to be put to sleep when it's the only way to end its suffering.' He glanced at her quickly. 'Don't look so sad. Think of it like this—as an animal lover you've chosen the best way to help them, by becoming a vet.'

For the rest of the journey Rose was silent as she reflected on the character of her companion. Everything about him appealed to her and she felt that in any trouble she could turn to him for help. If only she had not been obliged to start off on the wrong foot, by deceiving him about her involvement with Pete. Try as she might, she could not help feeling that Pete was going to be more and more difficult to keep at a distance.

At last, as David turned the car into the surgery drive, she forced her worries to the back of her mind and began to concentrate on the task that lay before her.

'You may need some help controlling this dog so I'll stay around in case I'm needed.' He opened the back of the car. 'He looks docile enough—a bit dopey, I think—but you never know with a dog like this who has been reared in such an environment. I'll carry him in.'

She watched as he talked soothingly to the injured dog, which made no resistance to the gentle hands doing the necessary. But his whole body trembled when he was placed on the examination table. With the nurses' help the anaesthetic was quickly and skilfully administered. It took half an hour to deal with the open wounds and bruises, then David came forward to carry the still unconscious dog to a recovery cage. Watching him carefully, David said, 'He'll do. Won't be long before he comes round. He really ought to be kept here overnight but, if you remember, his owners said they'd be here this evening to pick him up.'

Rose sighed. 'So he'll go back to his unhappy existence.'

David shook his head. 'We can't really be sure of that. We have suspicions but no proof. For all we know it may only be just an ordinary breeding establishment. I'll make a few discreet enquiries, although I'll have to be very careful. Anyhow, I'll be here when his owners come to fetch him so don't worry too much.'

Rose stiffened slightly. 'No need for that. We can deal with them, I'm sure.'

He laughed. 'I'm sure you can but I'd like to see them again. They might let out a little more information about their business.' He paused. 'I must be off now. Some calls waiting.'

When he had gone, the others, sensing a mystery, asked a few leading questions but Rose, taking her cue from David, gave no more information than was necessary.

Then, surprisingly, Penny said, 'I know that place. One of my boyfriends is something to do with the RSPCA and apparently they've got their eye on events that go on up there. He'll be very interested when I tell him about our latest patient.'

'Oh, dear!' Rose looked worried. 'I don't think you can tell him. It's this question of confidentiality.'

'Well, that may apply to vets but I don't see that we veterinary nurses are bound—'

'Of course we are,' Wendy said indignantly. 'You should know that.' She paused. 'In any case, if, as you say, the RSPCA are watching for anything suspicious then we can leave it to them. If it should come to a court case and they contact the vet who has dealt with the case we are at liberty to tell all we know.' She turned to Susan, 'That's right, isn't it?'

'Absolutely correct.' Susan smiled. 'So let's put it out of our minds for the present.'

Just before driving off, David put his head round the door. 'You'll be pleased to hear that I've got someone coming in before evening surgery. I'm pretty sure that she'll be ideal for the position of third veterinary nurse but I'd like you all…'' he smiled at them '…to give me your opinions when she's gone. Her name is Anna Norton and she comes from Shropshire.'

He went out to his car, leaving a stunned silence behind him. Susan was the first to break the spell. Laughing, she looked at Penny. 'So much for your hope that your friend would get the job. Isn't that just like David? Goes his own way then expects us to agree with him.'

Wendy shrugged. 'Well, it saves us a lot of trouble. If he says she's suitable then she probably is.'

Penny was indignant. 'He hasn't even interviewed anyone else. I think my friend would have been perfect for the position. He's altogether too autocratic, in my opinion.'

Susan laughed again. 'Well, perhaps that may stop you—as Wendy calls it—drooling over him. That is, unless you subconsciously like the autocratic type.'

Penny flushed. 'I've said before, I don't like the word "drooling" but perhaps you're right.' She paused. 'Anyway, if I don't like this Anna person I shall say so—not that it will make any difference unless, of course, you others don't like her either.' Gazing at them hopefully, she waited for their replies but their only reaction was that of amusement, which finally got through to her. She burst out laughing.

'OK, OK, so I'm making a mountain out of a molehill. Still, it has put me off David a bit.' She added thoughtfully, 'You must admit, he does act strangely sometimes. Look at his weird objection to married vets working in the same practice—it doesn't hold water. There are lots of flourishing practices run by husbands and wives.'

Rose stiffened slightly then hurriedly joined in as the others nodded their heads in agreement. She said cautiously, 'It's certainly a bit odd.' She glanced at Wendy. 'You've been here the longest—has he always held that view?'

Wendy said slowly, 'I really don't know, although once when he was talking about old Mr Barton— the former owner of this practice—he said that when Mrs Barton left her husband it was partly the old man's fault. She was a vet, too, and was kept as busy as he was. He said Mr Barton told him that was why they had never had children—no time for them—and that presumably could have been the reason that she left him.'

'Of all the crazy ideas!' Penny said scornfully. 'Surely there must be more to it than that.' She paused. 'Of course, it might be a kind of safety measure—you know, a protective barrier, in case any woman vet he employs should get ideas.' She grinned mischievously at Susan and Rose, who glanced at one another in stunned silence.

Then, as Susan collapsed into giggles, Rose said coolly, 'This conversation is getting a bit out of hand, don't you think? How about us getting back to work?'

An hour before evening surgery Anna Norton arrived, but without David. Tall, blonde and very pretty, she seemed rather embarrassed. 'Have I made a mistake in the time? Mr Langley said five p.m. but you say he isn't here. Shall I wait?'

Rose smiled. 'Of course. I expect he's been held up. Sit down and have a cup of tea. This is a quiet time for us.'

Anna looked at them with interest. 'Which of you is Rose? Mr Langley said the position involved working mostly for her.' Rose nodded and proceeded to introduce the others in turn.

As they assembled around the table Anna said calmly, 'I expect you'd like to know all about me. Well, I'm a qualified veterinary nurse and up till now I've been working up in Shropshire in my father's practice, but I wanted to come south for personal reasons.' She paused.

There was a short anticipatory silence, broken at

last by Penny. 'Too personal to tell us?' It had been an impertinent question and Anna flushed and hesitated.

Hurriedly Rose said, 'No need to answer that.' Then she proceeded to give a few details regarding the allocation of nurses' duties.

Penny, however, was not to be put down. She asked, 'Is it all fixed up with you and David? I mean, has he definitely taken you on?'

'David? Oh, you mean Mr Langley—well, yes, subject to only one thing.' She smiled a little uneasily, 'I suppose you can guess what that is.'

Susan and Rose said simultaneously, 'Us? Our approval—is that it?'

Anna nodded. 'Yes. It seemed a bit strange to me but he said quite definitely that he would ask you all for your candid opinion as it was most important that there should not be any friction in the practice.' She paused and looked at them almost appealingly. 'I don't see why there should be, do you? I'm not a quarrelsome person and you all seem very friendly.'

The only person who didn't respond with enthusiasm was Penny, who was evidently still smarting from Rose's rebuke, but even she stopped glowering eventually.

When at last David appeared, the atmosphere was relaxed and friendly. He joined in the conversation for a few minutes then asked Anna to wait in the office while he had a few words with the others.

As the door closed behind her he stood, looking

at them with raised eyebrows. At last he said, 'Well?'

To his obvious relief, they nodded approvingly and he said, 'Right.' Turning to Wendy and Penny, he added, 'There's a third bedroom in your bungalow so Anna can take that. She will start on Monday.'

Once more reassured, he went into the office, leaving them to finish their tea and get ready for evening surgery. Just before the first client was due, Pete came in and was immediately filled in with all the news by Penny. Before he had time to comment the office door opened and Anna came out, followed by David. He made the introduction and Rose watched with amusement as Pete's eyes widened in admiration.

What a good thing it would be if he should fall for this pretty blonde, she thought, and made a secret resolve to encourage him in that direction. Unless, of course… She glanced surreptitiously at Anna's left hand. No engagement ring. That was a relief. She smiled to herself then flushed guiltily as she met David's searching eyes. Annoyed with herself, she turned away to hide her embarrassment, only to hear him say quietly, 'Will you come into the office, please, Rose? I'd like a few words.'

CHAPTER THREE

SEATED opposite David, Rose waited while he assembled his thoughts. Smilingly she studied him and liked what she saw. He really was very attractive, she decided, but it was his character that intrigued her most. He was a kind man—of that she was sure—clever but not in the least conceited. That in itself was rare, she told herself as she compared him with other men she had known, in particular Pete.

Then she flushed as she realised the direction her thoughts were taking her. As she tried to dismiss them she knew her first impression of him remained. There was a hidden sadness behind those deep, searching eyes that aroused her curiosity, and it was not until he began to speak that she was able to clear her mind and pay attention.

He said, 'There are three things I'd like to discuss with you, but first I'd like your truthful impression of Anna Norton.'

She smiled. 'That's simple. I like her and I think she'll be easy to work with.' She paused. 'The others were of the same opinion.'

'Does that include Penny? I rather got the impression that she was a bit unwelcoming.'

Rose shrugged. 'You're very observant. Actually, Penny was a bit put out that you hadn't even considered her friend for the position.'

'So that was it.' He looked thoughtful. 'Well, I studied her CV and came to the conclusion that she moved around a bit too much for my liking. I want people who will stay with me and help build up the practice. Which brings me to the second thing I want to discuss. It's about Pete— Good gracious, you've gone quite pale. Does the mention of his name upset you? I thought you told me that it was all over between you.'

'It is.' Rose was angry with herself and therefore spoke sharply. 'You're imagining things.'

'Am I? Well, I'd better apologise, hadn't I?' His smile was gently mocking and Rose felt resentful. He had made her look foolish and she had an uncomfortable feeling that he knew she was hiding something from him. But the only secret she had kept concealed was that Pete had planned to deceive him. A plan in which she had refused to take part.

Having discovered in time that Pete was very devious and would do anything to get his partnership, she had the uneasy feeling that David should be warned. But that was something she could not bring herself to do. His voice broke into her worried thoughts.

'Do you think you could come out of that trance into which the mention of your former fiancé seems to have sent you?' He paused and his eyes grew cold as he watched the colour rising in her cheeks. He shook his head slowly. 'I have a strange feeling that you are hiding something unpleasant from me. I do hope that I won't come to regret having engaged two people who once were very close.'

He stopped for a few moments and then as she said nothing he added more kindly, 'If there is anything going on between you I hope you will eventually confide in me. Maybe I could help—come to some arrangement that would solve your problem.'

Now she was really angry—angry with Pete for having involved her in his deceit, angry with herself for not feeling able to tell David the truth and angry with David for being the cause of all the trouble.

Unable to keep silent, she said scornfully, 'There is no problem but if there were I don't see how you could possibly help. It's you having such a ridiculous phobia about married vets working together and being so suspicious of your employees that they hardly dare exchange a friendly word in case you think there is something going on between them.'

She regretted her words even as they poured out and as she saw the gathering fury in his eyes she realised she had done herself irrevocable harm. Well, there it was and half-defiantly she waited for his reaction. At first he seemed to have difficulty in finding words.

At last he said in a voice as cold as ice, 'A ridiculous phobia? Suspicious of my employees? Good God!' His voice grew harsh. 'Is this what a few casual words from me have led to? Made me out to be some kind of tyrant?' He paused grimly. 'I could, of course, give you a full explanation as to why I have this so-called phobia but I see no reason why I should have to justify myself to people who know nothing of my private life.'

His eyes grew colder in the short pause that

seemed to fill with a kind of menace, then he added, 'Up till now this practice has been a happy one and it makes me wonder if any trouble that now seems to exist is not due to the arrival of my two newest members of staff.' Ignoring Rose's indignant gasp, he went on ruthlessly, 'Especially in view of a talk I had recently with Pete. Yes, Rose, you may well look startled. I certainly was and I hope you will be able to explain his attitude towards you.'

At last she found her voice. 'I haven't the faintest idea what you mean. Pete has nothing to do with me.'

'So you say. In that case, why is he so anxious to get you out of the practice? No, wait—just listen. He came to see me, saying that as he is now halfway through his trial period he would like to know if his prospects of a partnership were still favourable. Fair question and I told him that I had no fears on that score. Then he stunned me by saying that he himself had one problem in that regard. That problem was you.'

He stopped when she exclaimed angrily, 'Me? What have I got to do with Pete's future? What on earth…?' She stared at him in genuine bewilderment, then gradually grew alarmed as he smiled cynically and shrugged.

'What indeed? Well, apparently he finds your presence too disturbing. He says he never wanted you to—as he put it—follow him here and, to put it bluntly, he wants me to choose between the two of you.'

Rose was aghast. This then was Pete's revenge

for her rejection of his schemes. She was in an impossible situation. At last she said very quietly, 'Well, it's up to you, isn't it?' She waited for his reply, anger boiling inside her at the thought of Pete's treachery and David's barely disguised doubts of her own story. Then, before he could answer, she added in a voice as cold as his, 'Like you, I can only say that I can see no reason why I should try and justify myself.'

'Touché,' he said grimly. 'As you say, it is entirely up to me. All the same I think you should have things out with Pete. Tell him that I have told you of his objections to your presence here then try to work something out between you.' He paused, then exclaimed, 'Good God, to have two people who were once engaged in the same practice is worse than anything I've ever had against two married vets.'

She said evenly, 'I can quite see that. It's obvious that one of us will have to go.'

He shook his head vehemently. 'Certainly not! From a veterinary point of view you are both ideal.' He glanced at his watch. 'Nearly time for evening surgery. Let's have a look at that bull terrier.'

Satan was waiting in the surgery and looking better, although his wounds were still very sore. Chained and muzzled, he was still very dopey and, as Wendy said, it seemed a pity he could not be allowed to spend another night in his warm, comfortable cage. Rose cast a quick glance round, which was intercepted by Penny.

'If you're looking for the new nurse, she's gone.'

She added grudgingly, 'She seems all right but I still think David could have given my friend a chance.'

Rose nodded sympathetically but her thoughts were far away. Somehow or other she must arrange a meeting with Pete—much as she disliked the idea. But first of all she must sort things out in her own mind and that required solitude. Meantime, she must concentrate on her work and not let indignant feelings distract her. A few minutes later the large, unpleasant man she had already met came to claim Satan, who gave him a pathetic welcome which brought a lump to Rose's throat.

Dogs were so trusting and loyal even when their owners were callous and uncaring. Presented with the account, the man began to bluster unpleasantly and, exactly on cue, David came out of his office. Rose stood by silently as he dealt firmly with their difficult client and finally, as he led his dog slowly out of the room, the man turned.

'Well, I shan't be coming here again. We're moving up north. There's too much talk about us down here—people like you, telling the police that we go in for dog fighting when all we do is breed bull terriers.'

Before David could protest the door was slammed and Rose said, 'Now we'll never know the truth. It may, of course, be that our suspicions are unjustified and that we've jumped to the wrong conclusion.' Then, without thinking, she added half to herself. 'It just shows how careful one should be.'

Turning away, she caught a glimpse of David's face as he stared at her grimly, and realised that he had taken her last remark personally. Well, let him, she thought angrily, and proceeded to take her turn with the new patients arriving in the waiting room. Dealing with a recalcitrant terrier, she heard David tell Wendy the list of his calls and sighed with relief as he left.

The little terrier was difficult to control and Penny came over to help. Holding him firmly, she laughed as Rose began her examination. 'It's funny how so very often these little ones are such toughies and the big ones are so much more amenable.'

Rose nodded ruefully as she gazed at the patches of eczema all over the dog's body. 'Well, I'm not surprised this poor little chap is bad-tempered. He must be in a constant state of irritation. I'll give him an injection, a special bath and some of that new antibiotic cream. Just look at all those fleas—let's deal with them now. Then I'd like to speak to the owner.'

Having tried to make the indifferent youth promise to follow her instructions, she sighed as he led the terrier away.

Penny looked at her sympathetically. 'It's depressing, isn't it? So many people neglect their pets almost to the point of cruelty.' She paused and smiled wryly. 'There's another problem waiting outside. A tremendously fat dog with a nasty smell.'

The owner and dog came in slowly and as soon as the Labrador's symptoms had been recounted Rose said, 'I'm pretty sure I know what's wrong but let me examine her first.'

With difficulty the enormous animal was hoisted

onto the table and she submitted docilely to Rose's careful examination and soothing words. At last Rose turned to the anxious owner and said, 'Well, it's a clear case of pyometra and she must be operated on in order to save her life. This condition is pus in the uterus—that is what is giving her this horrible smell.

'The problem is her weight, which must be greatly reduced before she can safely be given an anaesthetic. Do you think you could manage to stick to the diet I'll give you? A fortnight or maybe three weeks should bring her weight down enough for me to operate. In the meantime, I'll let you have some tablets, which will keep the condition under control for a while. Then it must be dealt with as soon as possible.'

She paused and added urgently, 'You really will stick to the diet, won't you? It's imperative that she loses some of this excessive weight. I know it will be hard for you to resist giving tidbits and she will look at you so appealingly that you will feel hard and cruel to refuse her. But you have to be cruel to be kind. She will soon get used to the new regime and as you see her getting her figure back you will have your reward of knowing that you are probably saving her life.'

Nodding slowly, her client looked rueful and said, 'I know you are right and I'll do my very best to help her.' She added, 'I live alone, you see, and I suppose I eat for comfort.' She smiled ruefully. 'Look where it's got me. Now you've given me the incentive I need. If I stop snacking all day Betsy won't be so tempted. I'll keep you informed of our progress.'

It was gratifying to have such a co-operative client, and as Rose continued with the rest of her patients she almost forgot her own troubles. As evening surgery drew to a close she checked on the appointments she had made for the next day—two cats to be spayed, a dog with a nasal papilloma, a parrot with beak trouble and a bitch with mammary tumours.

Looking round the surgery, she noted with pleasure that it was very well furnished with all the latest equipment, which certainly helped to ease the strain of difficult operations. Then she sighed as she recalled the confrontation with David. Mingled with anger was an uneasy feeling of guilt that she had deceived him. He had suggested that she should have it out with Pete and, on reflection, that seemed the obvious thing to do.

She waited until Wendy and Penny went off to their bungalow. She had smiled when they'd said they thought they'd better do a spot of tidying up in preparation for the arrival on Monday of what Penny called the blonde bombshell.

'She looks the type to be terribly organised, with a place for everything and everything in its place,' Penny had said mockingly.

But Wendy had said apprehensively, 'For goodness' sake, don't take it out on the poor girl just because David didn't choose your friend.' Still arguing, they had left Rose alone in the surgery.

For a few moments she hesitated then at last she

began to search for Pete's number. Tapping it out, she half hoped there wouldn't be a reply but he answered at once. She tried to make her voice sound casual as she said she would like to have a talk with him and suggested he should come to the surgery. There was a short silence before he said coldly, 'I've just come back from a heavy afternoon. I don't particularly want to turn out again so you'd better come over here.'

'OK.' She shrugged as she accepted his unwelcoming invitation, then bit her lip as he added, 'I'm surprised you want to have anything to do with me. What do you want to talk about?'

She hesitated then said, 'David has been telling me about—'

'Oh, he has, has he? And I suppose he told you that I don't want you in the practice if I get my partnership. Well, if that's what you want to talk about you can skip it. He had no right to tell you but I don't really care. That's the decision I've come to and you can make of it what you like. No point in coming over here to argue about it.'

'But, Pete,' she began, but he slammed down the receiver, leaving Rose on the verge of furious tears. Dashing her hand over her eyes, she turned away and saw David standing in the doorway. Defiantly she said, 'Well, that's what comes from following your advice and trying to have it out with Pete.' She paused. 'He's so furious he doesn't want to discuss anything.'

David's expression was hard to read as slowly he came towards her. She saw that his eyes were sympathetic, almost pitying. Before realising it, she found that his arm was round her shoulder as he said quietly, 'Rose, poor Rose. You really shouldn't have followed him here.'

Furiously, she glared up at him, astounded at his complete misunderstanding of the situation. 'I didn't follow him here in the way you seem to think.' She drew a long breath. 'I was the one who broke off the engagement, and now he is taking revenge by trying to get me out of this practice.'

His arm tightened round her and she felt herself being drawn towards him. He said softly, 'That's very natural. If I were in his place and had been rejected, I wouldn't be able to bear seeing you every day.'

She pulled herself away from him and said despairingly, 'That's not the real reason. You've got it all wrong.'

'No, I don't think I have.' He shook his head. 'I think you really want him back and that's why you were so upset just now.' He paused. 'You'll have to admit defeat eventually. I know it will be difficult—I've been through the same experience myself—but one day you'll meet someone else and then you'll wonder what you ever saw in Pete.'

She stared at him incredulously. At last she said hopelessly, 'You've got everything upside down. Why don't you believe me when I say I don't love Pete—never have, in fact—and didn't follow him here in order to get him back.' She paused. 'I know it looks like that but it isn't so. Please, believe me.'

For a few moments he gazed at her so searchingly

that she felt the colour rise and when he said coldly, 'Then why the hell *did* you come? There are plenty of jobs going for a girl like you.' Slowly he shook his head. 'I'm sorry, but I don't think you are telling the truth. Of course, it's really none of my business but I hate to see such self-delusion.'

It was too much. Furiously, she snapped. 'Men! You're all alike! You just can't believe that a girl could ever reject you. Your masculine ego twists everything round so that you always appear to be in the right.'

Suddenly she saw that he had gone very pale and that his eyes were blazing with anger. Then with one swift movement he reached out and crushed her in his arms. Hopelessly she battled to free herself but only managed to turn her head as he bent to kiss her. Ruthlessly he sought her mouth and, ignoring her gasps of protest, his lips came down on hers in a furious kiss that seemed to draw all the breath out of her body. When at last he released her she found that her legs were trembling so much that she reached out for a chair.

He pushed it forward, then said, 'Now what can I say?'

She was still breathless but stared at him in bewilderment. His kiss had disturbed her so much that she felt she could never forget it, but he seemed to think it was a mere lapse of control on his part.

She managed a shrug and at last said, 'I don't understand you and I'm certain that you have got the wrong end of the stick where Pete and I are concerned. You pity me because you think I have been rejected and have followed him here to try and get him back, but on the other hand you say that Pete is acting naturally because he is the one who has been hurt. So whose side are you on?'

'I'm not taking sides,' he said grimly. 'The fact is, I don't know what to believe. All I know is that I think I'm being deceived by you both and deceit is something I cannot tolerate.' He paused. 'I'm beginning to think that the two of you are playing a deep game and if I don't find out the truth soon I shall have to ask you both to resign from this practice.' As he turned towards the door he added very quietly, 'If I discover that you were really the innocent party I shall ask you to marry me.'

She gasped so violently that he stopped in his tracks, and the expression on his face was so incorrigible that she felt almost hysterical. As she tried to get control of herself she began to laugh until she found herself unable to stop. Suddenly she found herself being handed a glass of water. Taking it automatically, she gulped it down then handed it back.

Drawing a deep, calming breath, she said, 'That's, of course, a joke. A very poor one and in the worst possible taste.' She went on angrily, 'Sexual harassment by my employer. It comes under that heading, doesn't it?'

'Oh, definitely.' His tone was bitterly sarcastic. 'You'd be justified in making that allegation. It might solve all our problems.'

He turned and went quickly out of the room, leaving Rose in a state of utter confusion. Her first impulse was to go over to Pete's flat and have everything out with him but second thoughts took over. It would be better, she decided at last, to ignore everything—Pete's vengeful desire to get her out of the practice and David's angry suspicions that he was being deceived. Then her thoughts came to a dead stop. It had to be acknowledged—David *was* being deceived. She hadn't told him everything and when she had tried to explain he made it obvious that he didn't believe her.

In desperation she played with the idea of just walking out. After all, she wouldn't be leaving David in the lurch. Susan could manage on her own until someone else was engaged. She had done it before. That plan stayed with her for quite a while.

Back in her cottage she prepared a meal for which she found she had no appetite. At last, pushing her plate aside, she sat with her head in her hands, and tried to sort out her conflicting ideas.

Suddenly it all became clear. Yes, she would ignore everything and carry on with her work as though nothing had happened. Pete could continue making mischief, David could continue being suspicious—what did it matter?

She liked her work and there were outside interests she could cultivate in her spare time and probably these would lead to new friendships. Her spirits lifted and she was about to put on a tape to listen to while she cleared away her unfinished meal when the doorbell rang insistently.

For a moment she hesitated, fearing the caller might be Pete. Her heart was pounding when, at last, she opened the door, but to her utter amazement she

was confronted by David. Quickly recovering herself and remembering her new resolve, she said
lightly, 'Hello, this is a surprise. Is anything wrong?'

He shook his head. 'No, this is a personal call.
May I come in?'

Standing back, she waved him in and said calmly,
'Coffee? I was just going to make myself some.'

'Thank you.' His tone was stiff and her heart sank
but, determined to appear indifferent, she walked
past him into the kitchen and put on the kettle. As
she prepared the cafetière she realised that he was
standing behind her. Turning, she smiled at him
coolly. 'Why don't you go and sit down? This will
only take a minute or two.'

Obviously surprised at her casual attitude, he said,
'I've only come to apologise. No need to treat me
like a welcome guest. You must be furious with me
underneath that cool exterior.'

'Furious? Good heavens—I'd forgotten all about
it. We both lost our tempers—no point in dwelling
on what we said to each other. Water under the
bridge.' Pouring boiling water over the coffee, she
let it stand and placed two cups and saucers on a
tray, then asked, 'Milk and sugar?'

He said nothing and, turning, she saw that he was
staring at her incredulously. At last he muttered,
'Yes, please. Both—one sugar.'

Sitting opposite her in the living room, he stirred
his cup slowly, then placed it on the table beside
him. There was a short silence before he said
abruptly, 'Are you putting on an act for my benefit?'

As this was exactly what she was doing, she could

only laugh. 'Why on earth should I do that?' Seeing a flicker of anger in his eyes, she added with a trace of mockery, 'I think you're attaching too much importance to a foolish incident. Let's forget it, shall we?'

Picking up his coffee, he sipped it slowly with his eyes fixed on her. Putting down his cup, he said deliberately, 'That's very generous of you.' He added slowly, 'A foolish incident—is that all it meant to you?'

Her colour rose vividly but she managed an indifferent shrug. As she sipped her coffee she tried to obliterate the memory of the feelings he had aroused in her, feelings that she hadn't yet had time to analyse. At least that was what she told herself, knowing subconsciously that she feared to face what they might reveal. Searching desperately for a reply to his question, she was rescued from her dilemma by the sound of the telephone.

Thankfully, she picked up the receiver. Listening patiently to the agitated voice on the other end, she eventually wrote down a name and then said, 'Yes, of course I'll see him. Twenty minutes, you say? Right. Wrap him up warmly.'

Replacing the receiver, she turned to David. 'A cat whose tail has been caught in a slammed door. It sounds as though it is badly damaged—might even mean a small amputation. I must give the nurses a ring—I think Wendy is on duty this evening.'

'No need for that,' he said smoothly. 'I'm here. I'll do the necessary.'

She opened her mouth to demur, met his half-mocking look and contented herself with another shrug as they made their way to the surgery and began making preparations for a likely operation. When everything was ready Rose walked over to the window, ostensibly watching for the arrival of her patient. To her dismay David came and stood beside her, causing her heart to beat so violently that she felt sure he must hear it. Drawing a long breath, she calmed herself but he had noticed her agitation.

'Not nervous, are you? If you like, I'll do the op if it's necessary.'

She turned indignantly. 'Of course I'm not nervous. It's just that I—' She stopped abruptly. How could she say that it was his close proximity that made her feel uncomfortable?

He said smoothly, 'I expect you're feeling tired and probably hungry. I think we had better remedy that once this case is over.'

'If you mean that you are going to drag me out somewhere to eat then you're badly mistaken,' she said resentfully. 'I'm not a child. I'm quite capable of looking after myself.'

'More than capable, I should say,' he said smoothly. 'There's nothing of the clinging violet about you. You resemble your name. A beautiful, perfect rose, but protected by fierce thorns.'

She turned indignantly. 'You are talking a lot of nonsense.' She stopped at the sound of a car driving in, then added, 'Now, I must concentrate and so must you if you insist on staying here.'

The cat's tail was badly mangled and it was obvious that about an inch and a half would have to be removed. The owner, a middle-aged lady, had first to be reassured, calmed down and persuaded to return home and wait for a promised phone call as soon as the operation was over.

They worked quickly and quietly. David had charge of the anaesthetic machine and said nothing, even when Rose murmured occasionally to herself as she worked. Finally, the wound dressed and bandaged, the patient was placed carefully in a recovery cage. Picking up the telephone, Rose rang the cat's owner to tell her of the successful operation.

'Timmy should stay here for twenty-four hours,' she added, and suggested that his mistress should come in next morning to visit and reassure herself. At last, with a sigh of relief, she replaced the receiver and turned to begin cleaning up, only to find that David had put everything in order.

He turned from washing his hands and looked at her steadily. 'Let's put aside all animosity and go and have something to eat. There's a little place quite near here. I'm hungry and so should you be.'

She shook her head firmly. 'Thank you but no. I have all I want in my cottage.' She gazed around. 'As you've cleaned up, I'll say goodnight.'

'What about the cat?'

'You must have noticed that I put him in a portable cage. He's coming back with me so that I can keep watch on him.'

'Very well.' His voice was as cool as hers. 'Goodnight, then.'

Alone in the recovery room, Rose waited until she

was sure the cat was coming round safely then she carried him down to her car, placed the cage in the back and drove the short distance back to her cottage. All the time she was occupied she refused to allow her thoughts to dwell on David and the strange remarks he had made.

Even when she had finished her supper and was relaxing over her coffee, she managed to keep her mind free from thinking about either David or Pete, and spent an hour reading the *Veterinary Record*.

With the advent of the European Commission there were many new regulations to study, and drugs which had hitherto been the mainstay of all veterinary practice were constantly being withdrawn and others—sometimes not so efficacious—were being brought forward. It was all very frustrating. Sighing, Rose turned to examine the 'Situation Vacant' section at the end of the journal.

Her eyes widened as she saw the masses of demands for assistants all over the country. However, comparing these vacancies with the opportunities offered to her by David, she realised that she would probably find it difficult to match them with her future in this practice. This strengthened her resolve to put all her energies into her work and to avoid as much as possible all personal involvement with either Pete or David.

Pete was obviously going to do his best to get rid of her, but it was ultimately up to David to decide between them. However, if she made herself indispensable, Pete would fail and might even lose his chance of a partnership. Now that he had shown himself in his true colours she found that she no longer cared what happened to him.

Heartened by this discovery, she turned her attention to her patient who was conscious and in need of nourishment. He lapped up the milk she gave him and settled down to a good sleep. Stroking him quietly, she promised herself that if and when her future became secure she would get a pet for herself. There was no doubt about the theory that a loving relationship with an animal was very therapeutic.

Just as she began to tidy up, her eye was caught by an announcement in the *Record* that a meeting of Sussex vets was going to take place in a local hotel in a week's time. Her eyes brightened. Now that would be a good idea. She would have a word with David and if it was convenient she would take the day off in order to attend.

Next morning she went early to the surgery. As she came back out of the recovery room, after installing her patient there, she went in search of a tin of cat food. She realised that David was in the dispensary, filling his case with necessary drugs. He was muttering angrily to himself as he searched the shelves, then turned at her approach.

'These damned new regulations! Why do they have to do away with things we have used for years with satisfactory results?'

She shrugged. 'It certainly makes things difficult for us. I was reading about that very subject in the *Record*.' She paused. 'I see there is going to be a meeting of Sussex vets soon—I'd like to go. Would it be OK if I took my day off then?'

He nodded thoughtfully. 'Of course. As a matter of fact, I'm going myself so we can go together. I gave Pete the choice but he wasn't interested so he'll hold the fort for the farm work and Susan can manage on her own for a day. I'll pick you up at ten o'clock.'

He turned back to the drug shelf and found what he wanted. As he went out, he added, 'I'll be at Bells Farm for a good hour. Then I'll ring here to let you know where to find me next.'

As the door shut behind him Rose stood, biting her lip in exasperation. That was something she hadn't bargained on, and she wasn't sure if she was pleased or irritated to be spending a whole day in David's company when she had rather hoped to make some new friends. His presence would put a damper on that. On the other hand, it would show him that she was keen on her work and, after all, that was her newly formed plan.

As for Pete, well, it would be a small revenge for his underhand scheming. Nevertheless, she felt apprehensive at the prospect. The drive to their destination would only take about half an hour but what on earth would they talk about? The present atmosphere between them was decidedly stiff—well, there it was. It was all arranged and she couldn't possibly back out of it now.

Surgery that morning was very busy. Both she and Susan dealt with a variety of patients with diverse complaints. There had been rumours of parvo virus in a neighbouring town, and so many owners came in to have their dogs vaccinated that the supply of the necessary injection nearly ran out. A fierce tom-cat escaped from his basket in the surgery and caused a few minutes' panic. In the struggle to trap him Wendy's right hand was badly scratched.

A rabbit suffering from myxomatosis was brought in by a well-meaning but foolish woman who had picked it up as it wandered blindly across her path up on the downs. Told that it must be put out of its misery, she protested angrily and had to be assured that the disease was incurable and that to return the creature to the wild would only spread the infection. Only half-convinced, she went away muttering about 'callous vets'. Penny burst into tears and had to be consoled.

'The fact is,' Rose said sadly, 'some people just won't accept that death is preferable in many cases and that Nature herself is often cruel. Come on, Penny, cheer up. Misguided sympathy does more harm than good. It's mainly because rabbits are such pretty creatures that you felt upset. I bet if a crocodile came in with its mouth wide open you wouldn't balk at putting it to sleep.'

'I would if it was a baby croc,' Penny said defiantly. 'They are quite sweet. All animals are appealing—they're so helpless.'

Wendy laughed. 'Well, there is a youth in the waiting room with a young rat. They don't appeal to me. They give me the creeps.'

Rose nodded. 'Me too, but as it's probably a much-loved pet I'll do my best for it.'

It was indeed a pet and it had obviously been in a fight. Given an injection of antibiotic, it squealed

indignantly and was hastily returned to its affectionate owner. He was followed by a boy with a grass
snake in a cardboard box, which he placed on the
table and asked Rose to examine to make sure it
was healthy as he couldn't get it to eat.

'I found it on the heath,' he said gleefully. 'I'm
going to keep it as a pet.'

Rose shook her head. 'You can't keep it. You
should return it to the wild. It won't eat in captiv-
ity—you would have to feed it live food. Are you
prepared to feed it live frogs?'

The boy's face was downcast as he gazed long-
ingly at the snake, its green-brown skin glowing in
the sunshine. Then he looked up. 'Perhaps if I put
pieces of raw meat on a string and wiggled them he
might think they were alive.'

Rose shook her head again. 'You won't fool him
like that. You must take him back to where you
found him and let him live a natural life.'

Convinced at last, the boy promised to give the
snake his freedom.

Soon after that the staff sat down to coffee. A few
minutes later Pete joined them and listened as they
discussed their busy surgery.

Then he said, 'Well, that's nothing to what I shall
have next Wednesday. David will be going to a veterinary meeting so I shall have extra work. I can't
think why he wants to go. In my opinion these meetings are a waste of time, just an excuse for a get-
together and a good bit of drinking. They never
achieve anything much.'

Hastily changing the conversation, Rose brought

up the subject of the new veterinary nurse. Penny, obviously still harbouring some resentment over David's choice, said rather acidly that David had probably been persuaded by her good looks. Wendy said sharply that she shouldn't talk like that.

Soon after that Pete went off on more calls and Wendy said, 'He seems very disgruntled about David going to the veterinary meeting, doesn't he?'

Rose hesitated, knowing that she must mention her own involvement, then said calmly, 'Well, I shall see if he is right because I'm going with David.'

Wendy stared. 'Really? Well, that will be nice for you. Why didn't you tell Pete?'

Rose shrugged. 'I didn't want to start an argument.' Intercepting the curious glances that passed between the two girls, she added lightly, 'I was going anyway, and when I mentioned it to David he said we may as well go together. I'm not sure I wouldn't rather have gone on my own, but I had no option.'

'No option?' Penny looked sceptical. 'Good Lord! I'd give a lot for the chance of a day out with David. You don't know how lucky you are.'

Rose said sharply, 'It's not like that at all. It's work. We want to know more about the new regulations coming from Brussels.' She got up and went into the office, glad to get away from any more embarrassing questions, and frowned as she heard Penny's barely suppressed giggle. It was annoying to be subjected to these stupid insinuations, and for a moment she wondered if it might not be better to make some excuse and leave David to go on his own. After all, he could make all the necessary notes and one vet from each practice was all that was required. She would put it to him and see what he said.

He came in later that morning, and as he came into the office where Rose was working she tackled him straight away. He stared, then frowned. 'What's brought this on? I thought you were keen to go. You say your presence won't be necessary, but two heads are always better than one. Besides, we might well meet some old friends—surely you would like that?' He paused and looked at her searchingly. 'Or is it that you don't like the idea of spending the day with me?'

She flushed vividly. 'Don't be silly—of course that's not the reason.' Then, knowing that was a lie, she decided to speak the truth. She said half-laughingly, 'It's just that when I told the girls that I was going with you they put two and two together and made five.'

'Ah!' He nodded slowly. 'Well, I have the answer to that and it's, ''They say. What say they? Let them say!'''

She burst out laughing. 'I'll remember that.' She hesitated then sighed. 'OK, I'll come with you on Wednesday.'

CHAPTER FOUR

MONDAY morning saw the arrival of Anna Norton, the new VN. At first she seemed rather at a loose end as Penny and Wendy had hitherto divided their time very efficiently between Susan and Rose. Rose wondered why David had felt the need to take on another nurse. David himself did not appear at coffee-time but Pete came in with the obvious intention of making himself agreeable to Anna.

Sensing all their curiosity, she obviously decided to speak openly and, after talking about her last job up in Shropshire, she said casually, 'My father is a vet but he agreed with me that I should gain my nursing experience elsewhere. We get on very well but it's not a large practice and he's content with his present staff.

'Also...' Here she hesitated, flushed a little then said quietly, 'Well, there was somebody I thought I was in love with but it didn't work out, so when I saw this opening down here in Sussex I applied and here I am. A fresh environment and a new life.'

She smiled at them and, appreciative of her frankness, they all—including Penny—smiled back. The ice had been broken and Rose realised thankfully that David had made a good choice.

Wendy said, 'You're going to make things a lot

easier for us—it will mean that Penny and I will have more free time.'

Anna nodded. 'David told me that there was a possibility that he might open a branch practice. Is that so?'

'Good Lord.' Wendy and Penny stared open-mouthed and Pete looked up quickly. 'That's news to us. Did he say where and when?'

Anna shook her head. 'Oh, no. He just mentioned it in passing and I didn't like to ask. I got the impression that he rather regretted letting it slip because he immediately changed the subject. Do you know anything about it, Rose?'

Suddenly all eyes turned to Rose, and she felt a moment's panic. There was no alternative but to plead ignorance. She lifted her shoulders in a surprised shrug and said, 'It's news to me too.' She made a mental note to have it out with David later on. She had been put in a difficult position—obliged to tell another lie—and her resentment grew as she saw Pete staring at her suspiciously.

As far as she could remember, David had told her his plans for expansion in strict confidence so why had he been so foolish as to tell this to a newcomer? Still managing to keep up her act, she saw that Pete had turned his attention to Anna and that she was responding in a satisfactory manner. Seeing the glances passing between Wendy and Penny, she felt a sense of relief. It would be a good thing if Pete and Anna formed some kind of relationship—a thought that lifted her spirits as, coffee over, they all went about their various tasks.

She was in the dispensary when she heard Susan talking to a client. It was obviously an emergency as surgery had finished some while back. Then suddenly Susan came in, looking slightly flustered. 'Do you know anything about hedgehogs? Because I don't.' When Rose nodded, Susan breathed a sigh of relief. 'Thank goodness. I've got a young man here who has brought one in and he thinks it is wounded or sick and I haven't a clue how to treat it.'

The youth looked relieved when Rose came to look at the little animal on the examination table. 'I found it in our garden this morning. It doesn't look right to me.'

'It's quite young…' Rose put on her gloves and proceeded to search among its bristles. 'I'll give it an injection—it's got a touch of mange—and I'll also give the poor little thing some tinned dog food—it's very thin. People tend to put down bowls of bread and milk for hedgehogs but that is not really suitable food. We'll keep it here and if we can save it we'll send it to a rescue centre. There it will be cared for until it is fit enough to fend for itself.'

The young man gave a worried frown. 'That's going to take some time—I can see that.' He continued anxiously, 'The thing is, will I have to pay for all this treatment? If so, you'll have to put it to sleep now. I can't possibly pay—I'm unemployed and I know vets bills nowadays are frightful.'

The nurses looked at him sympathetically but Rose, flushing slightly at the accusation, said, 'I don't see that you are liable for any payment at all.

You brought in a wild creature, which was very caring of you, but you are not its owner so you are not responsible for it.'

She paused and smiled at his obvious relief, then added, 'As a matter of fact, there is a society called the British Hedgehog Preservation Society. I'll give them a ring and ask them to send any literature they have. If you'd like to call back in a few days, you can pick up any publications they send. You may find them interesting. In fact, I'll ask them to send several copies for us to put in the waiting room for other clients to read.'

Pleased that his rescue of the little creature had been so fruitful, the young man went away happy and Rose returned to her work, leaving the nurses in deep discussion about their unusual patient. Later, when David came in, she told him of her decision to treat the hedgehog. A little tentatively she added, 'I hope you don't think I ought just to have put it to sleep and not let the practice in for the expense of its treatment.'

'Good Lord, no. We're in the business of trying to keep animals alive. I certainly don't believe in bumping off wild animals just to save expense.' He smiled at her and, suddenly turning serious, he added, 'I met Pete out a little while ago—in fact, we dropped in at the pub and had a drink together.'

He hesitated for a moment, then looked at her searchingly and added, 'He seems to be rather taken with our new nurse—talked about taking her out some time soon. I thought I'd better warn you. I don't want you to be hurt.'

'Hurt? Good gracious, I won't be hurt. It's just what I want.' She frowned as she met his incredulous stare and added irritably, 'Oh, do stop linking us together. Pete and I are completely indifferent to one another. Not even friends now in view of his determination to get rid of me.'

David still looked puzzled. 'I just thought—' he began.

Rose butted in, 'Well, don't!' Her voice was sharp. 'Pete's private life is his own business and mine is mine. I like my job here and I do my best. I have no romantic entanglements whatsoever—and that should please you. My work will always come first.'

'A beautiful girl like you?' Now his voice was cynical. 'Do you expect me to believe that you are going to be celibate for the rest of your life?'

She flushed and turned away. 'You can believe what you like. In any case, you always twist my words so the fewer I say the better.'

Coming up behind her, he took her by the shoulders and forced her round to face him. 'Now, just listen to me. I want to believe you but you must admit that so far things have looked as though you have deliberately set out to deceive me.

'I have this feeling that you are hiding something from me—something to do with Pete and your so-called broken engagement. It was all just so convenient, wasn't it? As soon as you came here, I think, Pete told you of my objection to married vets working together in my practice.

'So the obvious thing to do, surely, was to pretend

there was nothing going on between you until Pete got his partnership. Then you would come out into the open, get married and I wouldn't have a leg to stand on. Pete's supposed interest in the new nurse and his declared wish to get you out of the practice may, for all I know, just be part of your plan to pull the wool over my eyes.'

Still holding her tight, he lifted her chin and tried to make her look him in the eye. Horrified at his correct assumption of Pete's original plan, her eyes filled with tears. How on earth could she ever explain so that he would believe her—believe her total revulsion of such a plan and her refusal to co-operate in this act of deception? But, in fact, she, too, had been guilty of deception in order to protect Pete. It was all too difficult and at last the tears fell unheeded down her cheeks.

'Oh, God! Don't cry—I can't bear it.' His voice shook for a moment, then suddenly he released her and said harshly, 'In any case, I've got my answer. You can't deny my accusations so you take refuge in a woman's ultimate weapon.'

'That's not true!' She wiped her tears away fiercely. 'It's because I despair of ever making you understand. You will never—' She broke off at the sound of the telephone and reached out automatically to answer it. She took a deep breath as David picked up the receiver first.

His face grew grim as he listened and at last he said, 'Well, you'd better bring him in now and we'll do what is necessary.'

When he turned back towards her she saw that he

was once again a veterinary surgeon with all personal concerns put aside. He said, 'This is a job we all hate. A perfectly healthy dog—four-year-old collie—who must be put to sleep. He has bitten three people quite badly and the owner fears for his small child.' He paused and looked at her tear-stained face. 'You're in no fit state to deal with it so I'll do it.'

'There's no need.' She managed to keep her voice steady. 'I can cope perfectly well. I'll ring for one of our nurses.'

'No need for that. I'll go and get everything ready while you see to your face.'

Rose shrugged resignedly and in a few minutes joined him in the operating theatre. He had already put out the Euthatal with a syringe beside the bottle. He said, 'I gather he's a large collie so we'd better lower the table. I'll restrain him, if necessary, then you can give the injection.'

With the table lowered, there was nothing more to do and the silence grew oppressive, especially as Rose could feel David's eyes on her as she moved towards the window. She drew several long breaths to calm herself and tried to fight back the memory of his accusation, which she knew she could never deny. All the same she longed to try and explain to him that she was an innocent victim of Pete's devious plans.

She sighed heavily. Then she saw a large car pull into the yard. A few minutes later a tall, well-built man entered with a beautiful collie, wagging his tail in a friendly fashion.

Handing over the lead to David, the man said, 'This is heart-breaking but I have no option. My wife is terrified Rufus will bite our little girl and so am I. His actions are quite irrational—one moment he's friendly and loving, then something seems to snap in his brain and he turns on the nearest person.'

He paused as he saw Rose take the lead from David and prepare to put the dog onto the examination table, then added, 'It's no use trying to find out what's wrong. I've been told by the police that I must have him put down. That's all you have to do. If you don't mind, I'll stay with him until he's gone.'

It was all over in a very short time, and with David's help the dog was carried out to the owner's car. Returning from the sad journey, David came back into the surgery in time to see Rose close the office door behind her. Pretending to work, she took up some papers and hoped he would take the hint and go away. But a few seconds later he stood in the doorway and, unable to ignore his presence, she half turned in her chair and looked at him questioningly.

He said quietly, 'That was very upsetting, wasn't it?'

She nodded, conscious that once more her face showed traces of tears and that his face was very pale. Swallowing hard, she said, 'I don't think I'll ever get used to putting a healthy animal to sleep.'

'Nor I,' he said. 'Now, look—it's lunchtime. Come and have something with me at the King's Head. I'll switch on the answering machine. The nurses will be back soon and they can put any messages through to my mobile phone. Please, don't shake your head. Try and put aside your obvious dislike of my company and share a meal with a hungry vet.'

She hesitated, then said slowly, 'Just as long as you keep our conversation confined to veterinary subjects. I don't think I can take any more arguing over my personal affairs.'

'Agreed.'

David held the door open for her, and as Rose reached for her jacket he took it from her and draped it over her shoulders. It was a small gesture but suddenly she felt a strange sensation that caused her heart to beat faster than usual. The protective way he placed the jacket round her and his courtesy in holding the door for her—simple, ordinary things, yet somehow they made her see him in a different light.

Used to Pete's casual rough-and-ready behaviour, she suddenly realised that there was a great gulf between the two men. Absorbed in her reflections, she kept silent until they entered the pub.

Seated opposite him at a table for two in a quiet corner, she studied him surreptitiously as she compared him mentally with Pete. Two totally different characters, she decided.

Pete was a good vet, both clinically and diagnostically, she had to admit, but his ruthless ambition often made him uncaring and callous.

David, on the other hand, was always compassionate and selfless, with a natural healing touch, treating every client as important as the next, whether they could pay or not.

This difference in their characters flowed through from their work to their personal lives in the way they treated their friends and colleagues.

She pondered on the way they behaved with her. David's spontaneously gentle manners were such a far cry from anything she had experienced with Pete.

'Well, aren't you going to eat anything?' David's voice broke into her thoughts and she flushed guiltily and glanced quickly down at the meal she had chosen. Picking up her knife and fork, she began to dissect the smoked trout, then looked up to meet his amused smile.

She said, 'Sorry, I was miles away. This trout looks very nice.'

'If I offered you a penny for your thoughts, would you tell me them?' His eyes were so searching that for a moment she could almost believe that he could read her mind, but, quickly dismissing the foolish idea, she said calmly, 'I wouldn't tell you for a billion pennies.'

He laughed. 'I hope you were concentrating on purely veterinary matters—remember, you made that a condition for coming out with me.'

Nodding slowly, she said evasively, 'Yes, veterinary matters were on my mind.' Then she smiled back.

He lifted his wineglass. 'Well, let's drink a toast to our work together.' As their glasses touched he added, 'I've been thinking seriously about the idea of a branch practice. My research has led me to two prosperous villages—Billington and Hurstlake—or, of course, there's old Mr Trent. Which would you prefer?'

Taken aback, she stared at him incredulously. 'What an extraordinary question!' She drew a long breath. 'Why ask me when not so long ago you made it clear that my future in your practice hung more or less on a thread?'

He nodded. 'Yes, I remember. I threatened to ask both you and Pete to resign if I didn't find out the truth about you. And then I said...' He paused. 'Do you remember what I said?'

She flushed hotly. 'Oh, yes, I remember. A stupid, wild statement that nearly sent me into hysterics. It still makes me laugh.'

His eyes glinted at her mockery. 'Just so. Well, putting that aside for a moment, will you come out with me one evening and tell me which, in your opinion, would be a suitable place to set up a branch practice?'

She shook her head firmly. 'No. I don't consider it's anything to do with me.'

'It might well be.' He looked at her steadily but she shook her head again and turned her attention to her plate until at last she pushed it aside.

'That was very good,' she said calmly. 'No, thanks, I don't want any coffee.' She glanced at her watch. 'I must go now. Lots of things to do.'

Once back in the surgery she found his last words echoing in her mind. 'Don't forget the veterinary meeting on Wednesday.' She wondered whether or not to make some excuse and thus avoid a whole day in his company. If that was impossible, then her best plan would be to circulate among the other vets whenever there was a break for discussion.

Wednesday promised to be a perfect spring day, warm and sunny with a light invigorating breeze coming from the sea. As David and Rose drove along the coast road David said, 'It will soon be warm enough to go swimming. You must let me show you a little beach right away from the crowds. It's at the foot of the cliffs—we're coming up to it now.' He pulled up and indicated a narrow path winding down the cliff side. 'It's called Smugglers Bay and so it was in the old days.'

Rose gave a little shudder. 'I don't like the look of that narrow path. There's nothing to hold onto, and as I'm not too good with heights I think I'll give it a miss and just swim in the usual place. I'll go early in the morning before the beach gets too crowded.'

'Oh, but there is a rope handrail on the cliff side—you can't see it from here. It's really not as difficult as it looks. You must let me take you there one day in the summer.'

She made a quick calculation. 'I might not be here in the summer.' She instantly regretted her impulsive remark and added quickly, 'Let's avoid that subject, shall we? I want to enjoy myself today. I'm hoping I'll meet a few old friends.'

His voice was dry. 'Male or female?'

'Both. I made lots of friends at veterinary college.

I'm sorry I lost touch but somehow I never seemed to have the time to contact them.'

'Well, of course, being engaged to Pete must have made it more difficult.'

That was too near the truth to be comfortable and Rose instantly changed the subject by bringing the conversation round to the veterinary meeting. 'Do you think talking about the new European directives will achieve anything?'

'Let's hope we'll be able to make our voice heard, though...' He paused and added cynically, 'I expect that eventually the discussion will turn to the subject of profits. Money is becoming all too important in our profession.' He smiled cynically. 'I won't be too popular when I say this, will I?'

She laughed.

'Exactly. All the same,' he went on, 'I don't like charging high fees for quite simple treatments—in fact, I'm thinking of going against the trend and reducing them. Consultation charges, for instance—why should people have to pay as soon as they put their foot over the threshold? They love their pets and want to do their best for them and it is a compliment to us when they seek our advice.'

Rose said warmly, 'I couldn't agree with you more.'

Pleased with her approval, he turned quickly to smile at her. Suddenly all stiffness between them vanished, the bright day seemed even brighter and when David turned on the radio they sang along to the music.

On arrival at the King's Head David came round

to open the door for her and said softly, 'I'm so glad you came with me.'

Her heart gave a little jerk at the look in his eyes, and her feeling of euphoria lasted throughout the meeting. Her original wish to encounter old friends was granted, which was pleasing, and David brought several of his friends over to be introduced to her, watching quietly at the evident admiration she received.

Congratulated several times on his beautiful assistant, he assented and laughed when she was told that if at any time in the future she felt like a change of employment there were many practices that would welcome her with open arms.

Many plans were put forward to combat various directives that went against all previous usage but when David put forward his scheme for reducing fees charged to clients it met with only subdued enthusiasm.

When at last it was all over and they began to disperse, a voice from behind them made them both stop and turn. A tall, fair-haired man pushed his way forward.

'Rose! By all that's wonderful!' He put out his hand then bent down and kissed her lightly on the cheek.

Subconsciously Rose felt David stiffen beside her as she returned the kiss and said delightedly, 'Richard! What a nice surprise! It's years…'

'Yes, well, when you got engaged to Pete I gave up the chase and took a job as far away as possible—Scotland, in fact. I'm down here on a visit to my mother and at the same time I'm looking around for a practice to buy. I like this part of the world. But what about you? I suppose you and Pete are—' He glanced quickly at David and Rose took the hint and made the necessary introductions.

David said calmly, 'You look puzzled. The fact is, both Rose and Pete work for me.'

'Oh!' Richard looked even more bewildered and turned to Rose. 'I rather thought you and Pete would have set up on your own once you were married.'

Rose felt herself flushing but she managed to say steadily, 'We're not married. We broke up some time ago.'

'Good Lord! If I had known that…' He paused. 'Then is the field open? You're not tied up with anyone else?' He stopped again then shook his head slowly. 'So how come you're both working in the same practice? Surely that's a bit awkward?'

'It's a long story.' Rose glanced around. 'Too many people here wanting to get by and we have to get back.' She began to edge away but Richard looked dismayed.

'You can't go off like that. We must meet again soon. I'll ring you and we'll be able to talk over old times. I shall be down here for some time. I'm hoping to buy a practice not far from here—an elderly man who is about to retire.' He turned to David. 'Perhaps you know him—Mr Trent. His practice has been running down for some time so if I get it I will have to build it up.'

'I doubt if you will get it.' David's voice was cool. 'As a matter of fact, I've got first refusal.'

'What? He never told me there was anyone else after it—cunning old devil.' Richard paused. 'Still, I'll hang on. Perhaps you'll change your mind. Thinking of it as a branch practice, are you?'

David nodded steadily. 'That's the general idea. But if I do change my mind I'll let you know so that you'll have second refusal.' He paused and put his hand lightly on Rose's shoulder. 'We must be off.'

'Wait a moment. Rose, your telephone number, please.'

She gave it quickly. 'That's the practice number but you can have my private number if you would like.'

'Of course I would.' Richard wrote it down and added as they moved away, 'Well, it's rather bad news about Mr Trent's practice, but it's marvellous meeting you again.' Then with a grin he added, 'What's more, Pete no longer stands in my way. I'll call soon!'

As soon as they reached the car David held the door open and waited as she got in, looking down at Rose with an expression that she found puzzling.

'Well, well,' he said. 'An admirer from your past. Looks as though he means business. I'll have to watch my step.'

She eyed him warily. 'What can you possibly mean? You told him you had first refusal on Mr Trent's practice so there's no need to fear he'll be a professional rival.'

He laughed shortly. 'You know very well what I mean.'

Pulling on the safety belt, she said nothing, waiting until he had settled himself behind the wheel before she said slowly, 'I suppose I do, but I don't understand you. You come out with such strange remarks. For instance...' She paused, biting her lip.

As he released the handbrake he turned and looked at her steadily. Then he grinned. 'You're referring to my statement that I would marry you?'

'Yes. Your idea of a joke, I suppose. A pretty stupid one, too. Then you told me in confidence about the branch practice and the next moment you blurt it out to Anna. When she told the rest of us and they all asked me if I knew anything about it, I lied and pleaded ignorance. I don't like telling lies.'

He nodded slowly. 'I see your point. Well, you deserve an explanation so let's talk about it over lunch.' He paused. 'I tell you what—let's have a quick snack somewhere, then whip over to Mr Trent and I'll show you the practice I'm interested in.'

'The one that Richard has his eye on?' She looked at him scornfully. 'Has the fact that he wants it made you even keener to buy it?'

'You may be right.' David's mouth twitched at the corner. 'I certainly wouldn't like it to go to a possible rival.' He paused and added softly, 'In both senses of the word.'

'There you go again. Another ridiculous statement.' She snapped, 'A few words from a complete stranger and you start insinuating goodness knows what.'

He made no answer and it wasn't until they were seated at a table in the first pub they came to that he said quietly, 'You say you don't understand me so I'd better make myself clear. First of all, I make up my mind quickly—sometimes too quickly for my own liking—but experience has taught me that my first impressions are usually right. Now, when I first saw you I was shaken to the core.

'Here, something told me, was the only girl in the world for me. No matter that there was a mystery about her, no matter that she was obviously hiding something and that there was another man in her background. I just knew that eventually…you would be my wife.' He stopped, shrugged and added calmly, 'It's known as love at first sight.'

Rose stared at him incredulously, drew a deep breath and opened her mouth, but no words came. He smiled ruefully, took up his glass and drank quickly, his eyes fixed on her for a long moment. Then he gave a short laugh. 'I suppose you think I'm mad—well, in a way I am. Madly in love—a condition that has knocked me sideways.'

At last she found her voice. She said unsteadily, 'Yes… You're right—you must be crazy.' Pushing her chair back, she got to her feet. 'Of all the arrogant, self-absorbed speeches I've ever heard, that takes the biscuit. You would have done better to have kept it to yourself.' Turning away, she went out to his car and stood, waiting, until he joined her. Then she said, 'Don't bother to drive over to Mr Trent's practice. I'm not interested.'

'Good God!' He stood, car keys in hand, staring at her incredulously. 'What have I done wrong? I thought—'

'Yes—you thought I would be flattered. Even grateful. Well, I'm not. I'm just astounded at the way in which my feelings are totally ignored. Well, let me tell you that I, too, make up my mind quickly. I shall be leaving here in a month's time. Now, will you please take me straight back to my cottage?'

She saw his face whiten and his mouth set in a grim line, but he said nothing and the silence between them lasted until they reached their destination.

As he pulled up he said calmly, 'I'm sorry. I expressed myself badly.' He paused. 'Will you please forget my outburst? I won't embarrass you again.'

Struggling with her seat belt, which seemed to have got entangled, Rose made no answer. Suddenly as he reached out to unravel it she felt the pressure of his arm and a shock ran through her. He also must have felt it for he drew back quickly and held the door open for her to get out. Pulling herself erect she looked David full in the face.

'I can't forget and I'll have to leave. You must see that I couldn't possibly work with you after this.'

'There's no need to be so melodramatic. I've said I won't bother you again.'

She shrugged. 'Maybe, but my decision stands. Another month and I'll leave.'

'Well, I'm not the only one who is crazy. Throwing away the prospect of a leap forward in your career just because of a few ill-chosen words from me. Come on, Rose, forget I ever said them. It was clumsy of me, I admit. I should have waited until you were established as my partner and in charge of the branch practice.'

She looked at him scornfully. 'More ill-chosen words. And if I had been so foolish as to consent to be your wife, what then? My career as a vet would come to an end, wouldn't it?'

He looked puzzled. 'What do you mean?'

'I thought you were prejudiced against married couples working in the same practice.'

'Oh, that!' He shrugged, then he said thoughtfully, 'It's the children, you see. I myself suffered as a result of both my parents working as vets. I was sent to boarding school at the age of seven—can you imagine how homesick I was? The feeling that I wasn't wanted, especially as very little interest was shown in my school life. Both my parents were always too busy to visit me.' He paused.

'Well, that's water under the bridge now, but when I grew old enough to think about it I resolved that no child of mine would suffer because its parents—and in particular its mother—had no time for its emotional needs.'

Against her will Rose was moved. She said quietly, 'I suppose that's understandable but I think nevertheless that you are wrong. All the same...' she began to move away '...it's nothing to do with me.'

She heard him drive away as she shut her door and went slowly into her kitchen. In the middle of making some tea she stopped. Now she really had to find another job. For a moment desolation swept over her as she drank her tea, but she pulled herself together. It shouldn't be too difficult.

Picking up a copy of the *Veterinary Record*, she scanned the pages of vacancies and considered the most attractive ones, trying to ignore the regret that she had been so impulsive. But she was sure that David didn't mean what he said. Was he just trying to distract her from Pete?

Suddenly the telephone rang and automatically she picked up the receiver—and found herself talking to Richard. A few minutes later she replaced it and went to pour herself another cup of tea. It seemed that Fate was taking a hand in her affairs.

Laughingly Richard had admitted that he was head-hunting, trying to lure her away from David's practice. But she hadn't told him of the prospects David had promised. Neither had she told him of her own decision to reject them, but she had consented to have dinner with him in two days' time and talk it all over.

CHAPTER FIVE

ROSE awoke next morning heavy-eyed, but luckily the day was uneventful. Even evening surgery was quiet and she went back to her cottage, intending to have an early night. She was just finishing a light meal when the telephone rang. David's voice was tense.

'Do you know where Pete is? Wendy tells me she had tried him on his mobile without luck. It's his night on duty and there is a difficult calving at Underwood Farm—probably an abnormality.' He paused. 'Is he with you?'

'No, he isn't,' Rose said curtly, 'Nor is he likely to be.'

'Sorry. Well, the alternative is that he has taken Anna out. Apparently she isn't around either.' Rose waited while he drew a long breath, then he said, 'It looks as though I'd better go myself.' He added tentatively, 'I suppose you wouldn't like to join me? It seems an interesting case.'

Completely forgetting that she was still at loggerheads with David, she agreed eagerly, and soon was seated in his car, talking of the possible outcome of the case awaiting them.

As they passed the village pub she stopped speaking abruptly, staring at the car parked outside. Surely that was Pete's car? Hastily she began to talk again but it was too late. David slowed down and reversed a few yards. Rose was silent as he pulled up and stared at the empty car. After a moment he shrugged and accelerated away.

Glancing at her, he nodded and said grimly, 'Pete's in that pub without doubt.'

'Well, aren't you going to confront him and send him to Underwood Farm?'

David's voice was cold. 'No, I'll speak to him tomorrow. This case is urgent. Already too much time has been wasted.'

It was getting dark when they arrived, and Mr Fison was none too pleased when they walked into the cowshed. A few words of explanation did very little to appease him as he waited for David to pull on his obstetric gown. Mr Fison said to Rose, 'Well, if you're here to assist you won't be much use dressed like that. Haven't you got an overall?'

She flushed but David came to her rescue.

'There's a rubber gown in the car.' As she turned to fetch it she heard him say, 'We've had a veterinary meeting. That's why we're late. Now let's look at this poor animal.'

By the time she returned David was on his knees with his right arm inside the cow. She stood, waiting silently, until at last he rose to his feet.

'I think it is either Siamese twins or one large calf with extra limbs. Whatever, it's already dead. I shall have to get it out bit by bit. She's already exhausted by long straining so I'll give her a local anaesthetic and see if I can avoid doing her an injury.'

As Rose prepared the injection the farmer looked

at her curiously. 'Don't you think you'd better go back and sit in the car? This is going to be very grisly—not fit for a girl like you to watch.'

Rose held back her resentment with difficulty. She said stiffly, 'Mr Fison, I'm a fully qualified veterinary surgeon.' Turning to David, she began to discuss the case in technical terms, leaving the farmer looking very discomfited. It was a long job and several times Mr Fison turned away as David gently placed the dead calf on the straw. After attending to the mother, David said, 'I think she'll be OK now but I'll come in tomorrow to make sure.'

When at last they drove away David grinned. 'Just a few words and you put him properly in his place. I must say, I held my breath and waited for an explosion on your part. Instead, you were magnificently dignified. I'm sure that's the best way to deal with these chauvinistic farmers. There are still quite a few left.'

'Thankfully, not a lot,' Rose said, and then ruefully she added, 'Actually, it was a horrible case, wasn't it? A deformed calf and the mother had such a hard time.'

He glanced at her quickly. 'I think we could both do with a drink. Let's pull in at the next pub.'

To Rose's relief it was not the pub where they had seen Pete's car, and they were soon settled at a table. She watched as David went to buy the drinks. She looked at him compassionately when he joined her.

'You look very tired. Have you hurt your back?'

He grinned ruefully. 'A bit, but nothing that a hot

bath won't put right. Thankfully, I'm pretty fit.' He drank deeply and added, 'I suppose this is as good a place as any to tell you of my future plans. I'm—'

'No,' Rose said firmly. 'You're too tired and so am I. Leave it for the time being.' She paused. 'About the cow—will you go and see it tomorrow or will you pass her over to Pete?'

Seeing his mouth tighten, she rather wished she hadn't asked the question, but it was too late. He said sharply, 'She's my patient now so, of course, I'll check her over tomorrow. As for Pete, I'll sort him out at the earliest possible moment.' He paused. 'I'm sorry, Rose, but he was on duty and he should have been on call.'

'Well, of course.' She looked puzzled. 'I don't know why you are apologising to me. I don't want to shield him—he's not my responsibility.'

'So you say.' He gave her a quick glance. 'Don't you resent his sudden interest in Anna?'

'No,' she said calmly. 'Why should I?'

'Oh, I don't know.' He shrugged. 'I'm still uncertain about your relationship with Pete. I can't help feeling that there's something hidden from me.' He put down his drink and gazed at her steadily. 'Is there, Rose?'

She could feel the colour drain from her face. How could she say truthfully that she had been absolutely frank with him? At last she said evasively, 'I've already told you that I'm no longer engaged to Pete. That it was all a mistake. What more is there to say?'

He sat silent, obviously disappointed by her answer. His expression was almost sad, and she felt a pang of regret that she couldn't tell him more. She dared not tell him that she had originally been party to a certain amount of deceit when deceit was what he hated and despised.

Suddenly he said coldly, 'Have you finished your drink? I think we should make a move.'

On the way back he slowed down as they passed the pub where Pete's car had been parked, but it was no longer there. He gave an almost imperceptible shrug as he accelerated again, but made no comment. Only the set of his mouth and the way his hands tightened on the steering-wheel betrayed his annoyance.

Rose murmured almost to herself, 'If only Pete had kept in touch with the nurses, it wouldn't have been so bad.'

He glanced at her grimly. 'Making excuses for him, are you? Very noble, but I should have thought the fact that he took Anna out would have mattered to you personally.'

'Oh! Good grief!' Rose drew a long exasperated breath, 'I don't care how many girls he takes out. I was thinking of the risk he was taking when he is still on probation with you.'

'Well, there you are. Still concerned for his welfare.' David's laugh was scornful and with rising indignation Rose was about to answer angrily, then thought better of trying to make him understand.

'What's the use?' She shrugged indifferently. 'You can think what you like. I see no need to justify myself to you. You are only my employer, not my psychiatrist. Not,' she added sharply, 'that I need one.'

He burst out laughing and for a moment she felt like joining in. Still irritated, however, she added, 'And I haven't forgotten that, like Pete, I'm also on probation.' Then suddenly she remembered. 'At least, no longer. I'm leaving at the end of the month.'

His laughter died. 'True, but I'm hoping you will change your mind about that. As a veterinary colleague you have become indispensable to me. So, please, will you think again?'

'Well…' She hesitated. 'I might.' But her voice was cold as she added, 'Only I'd like you to remember that my personal life is entirely separate from my work.'

'I'll try and remember,' he said quietly, and withdrew into a silence which lasted until they reached her cottage. As the car came to a halt, he said, 'We'll have to arrange another time to talk. Thank you for coming to help tonight.'

Suddenly, leaning towards her as she began to undo her safety belt, he kissed her gently on the cheek—a kiss to which she could not possibly object—and she went indoors, trying to stifle an unexpected desire that his kiss had been more fervent. The feeling persisted, however, and her dreams that night were troubled.

The morning surgery was busy next day, and when it was over Rose sat down with a sigh of relief to a welcome cup of coffee.

Wendy was curious. 'Did you enjoy the meeting on Wednesday?'

Rose shrugged. 'It wasn't all that interesting. Not nearly as interesting as the visit to Underwood Farm.'

Suddenly remembering that no one knew she had gone with David, she cut short her description, but it was too late.

Anna looked up shortly and said, 'Why did David have to go? He wasn't on duty.'

'No, but Pete couldn't be contacted.' Rose saw the distress on Anna's face and added gently, 'Someone had to go—it was an emergency.'

Wendy said accusingly, 'I had to call David out eventually. You were with Pete, weren't you? At least that's what we supposed.'

Anna nodded. 'Yes, but he said it would be all right. He said he could be contacted on his mobile phone.'

'Well, we tried his mobile again and again without success. It was obviously switched off.' She shrugged. 'He's in trouble but you are not to blame.'

Anna sat, frowning thoughtfully. Then she said, 'Well, I must say, if he switches off his mobile when he is on call he deserves whatever he's got coming to him. If one of my father's assistants had played that sort of trick he would have been for the high jump. I shan't tell my father, of course, because that would put him against Pete and ruin his chances—' Suddenly she bit her lip and added quickly, 'Forget I said that, will you, please? It's supposed to be a secret.'

There was a long silence, which was broken at last by Susan. 'Well, you've said enough to make us deadly curious. Come on, tell all. Why on earth should it matter to your father? Unless, of course, Pete is hoping for a job in his practice.'

Anna's voice trembled. 'I asked you to forget what I said.' Getting up, she went to the door. 'I'll be in the recovery room if I'm wanted.'

Penny opened her mouth to speak but Rose forestalled her. 'Cut it out, Penny. It's nothing to do with us. Let's get on with our work.'

For half an hour Rose worked steadily in the office. She heard the telephone ring several times but no one called her out and she was left in peace. Her task completed, she put her papers in order and was about to get up when the door opened and David came forward.

'Do you mind, Rose? I'm sorry to disturb you but I want to have a word with Pete in here.'

Getting up hurriedly, she caught a glimpse of Pete then left, without catching either man's eye. Shutting the door quietly behind them, she went into the dispensary and spent some time checking the drugs.

Suddenly the telephone rang and an agitated voice told her about an unconscious dog. It had been hit by a lorry and sent spinning into the gutter in full view of its owner. The lorry driver had carried it into her house.

Taking the name and address, Rose was pulling on her jacket when the office door opened and David and Pete came out. The latter's face was sullen and

David's expression unreadable. Hurriedly she told David where she was going, but to her surprise he shook his head.

'No need for you to go. I've nothing urgent on at the moment.' He turned to Pete. 'Take my routine visit to the Hedge Piggeries, will you, please?'

Rose said coolly, 'There's really no need for you to go. I'm perfectly capable of dealing with an unconscious dog.'

'Never said you weren't.' David grinned. 'But I'm going nevertheless.'

Rose flushed and handed over the address. 'Well, you're the boss. You can do whatever you wish.'

'Not everything,' he said softly, and left her staring after him.

Penny and Wendy made all the preparations for the reception of the emergency patient, supervised by Susan. Rose went into the recovery room to have a look at a cat who was making too slow a recovery from the anaesthetic given that morning. After giving it an injection of Mylophyline to stimulate its heart, she turned to speak to Anna who was standing by the window.

To her surprise she saw that Anna had been crying and looked so pathetic that Rose put an arm round her. 'For goodness' sake, what's wrong? Aren't you well?'

Anna's voice was choked. 'It's nothing you can do anything about. It's purely personal.'
Rose hesitated, then asked tentatively, 'Pete?'

Anna nodded reluctantly, then wiped her eyes and

said, 'I'm worried about him.' She swallowed hard.
'You can probably guess that I'm in love with him.'

'Oh, dear,' Rose said inadequately, then stayed
silent as Anna drew a long breath in an effort to pull
herself together.

Looking at Rose steadily, she said, 'You were engaged to him once, weren't you? Did you break it
off or did he?'

'I did.'

'Why?'

This was too much. Rose shook her head then,
seeing Anna's eyes filling with tears again, she said
hastily, 'I realised that I didn't love him.'

'Pete says—'

'Never mind what Pete says,' Rose chipped in
quickly, trying to quell her rising resentment. 'Look,
I think this conversation has gone far enough. Now,
if you don't want David to see you've been crying,
I think you'd better disappear for a while. I'll say
you are feeling a bit off colour.'

With a quick glance out of the window Anna said,
'He's just driving in now. I'll go back to the bungalow.'

Followed by the dog's anxious owners, David
came in and laid his patient on the examination
table. Rose turned to the two worried faces.

'You've had a terrible shock. I'm sure you could
do with a cup of tea. We've put the kettle on so,
please, sit down. What is your dog's name?'

The woman said, 'We're the Robinsons and he…'
she nodded towards the table '…is our beloved
Bobby. Do you think…?' she faltered, near to tears.

Rose said compassionately, 'We'll do our best.'
Susan came in and she and Rose watched carefully
as David began his examination. At last he looked
up, his face very serious.

'He's bleeding internally so we'll give him a
blood transfusion. If that works we can see to those
back legs, which are both broken, but he is in no
state for a general anaesthetic so that must wait a
while. He is badly shocked and I'm afraid it's touch
and go as to whether he'll make it.'

He paused, seeing the Robinsons' stricken faces.
'The best thing you can do is to go home and wait
for my telephone call.'

When they had gone and the transfusion had been
set up, they stood silently, waiting and watching.
But it was all in vain. In spite of their efforts to keep
the dog alive, it was plain to see he was sinking fast.
At last his breathing grew fainter until it stopped.
After a final try to revive him, a grim-faced David
went to the telephone. He returned, looking a trifle
pale and shaken, and Rose's heart went out to him.

It was always sad to lose a patient but telling the
owners, that was a traumatic experience. He went to
the window and stood staring out unseeingly for a
few moments.

As the others went out of the room, Rose said
quietly, 'You did your very best. You mustn't blame
yourself.'

He turned and she saw his eyes were full of tears.

'One always does. One always feels so inade-
quate. Giving the bad news to the owners is the
hardest thing of all.'

'How did they take it?'

'Very upset.' He sighed. 'Blaming themselves for having let Bobby get out into the road. Someone had left the gate open and Mrs Robinson had rushed out to close it but too late. Bobby had seen another dog across the road and a lorry hit him far and square.'

'He braced himself, drew a long breath and said, 'Well, there it is. A thing we have to take in our stride.' He paused and gave a wry smile. 'At least you won't have to break your date with Richard to-night, anyway. This patient hasn't wasted much time, has he?'

To her annoyance she felt herself flushing under his sardonic gaze. 'I'd completely forgotten.'

He shook his head disbelievingly. 'Well, enjoy yourself. Judging from what he said when you met, he's not going to let the grass grow under his feet.'

'I don't know what you mean.' Rose was indignant. 'He's just an old friend.'

'You know very well what I mean. But just don't forget that you are still employed here.'

Rose's retort was sharp. 'If you mean by that that I am going to give him details of the way you run your practice, you're completely wrong. You should know me better than that.' Glowering at him, she saw that his mocking expression had disappeared.

He said quietly, 'That was not my meaning at all. What I fear is that he will try to persuade you to throw in your lot with him.'

The thought had never occurred to her but suddenly the idea seemed rather attractive. Watching the effect of his words, David saw the flash of interest in her eyes.

Frowning, he said, 'That struck a cord, didn't it?'

There was a long pause, then Rose shrugged and looked at her watch. 'I must get on.'

'There's nothing that won't wait till tomorrow.' His voice was cool. 'I'll take evening surgery with Susan. Then you won't have to keep Richard waiting.'

The idea that Richard might want her to join with him in setting up a practice stayed with her for the rest of the afternoon. Of course, he might want more than a veterinary partner. He was undeniably attractive but she had never been in love with him, nor was she ever likely to be.

On the other hand, there was David, whose attitude towards her was strangely possessive. Remembering his impulsive statement about wanting to marry her, she was puzzled in the extreme. Was it just a joke or was he in earnest? And how did she feel about him? The fact that her heart pounded when he was near could be put down to a feeling of guilt at having deceived him, however innocently, but somehow she knew it was more than that.

Her feelings for him were ambiguous, so confused that she hardly dared examine them closely. Accordingly she pushed them aside, promising herself that she would think about them later when she had more time.

The rest of the day was uneventful and with no evening surgery she made her preparations in a leisurely fashion. At intervals she paused, wondering why she was taking so much trouble with her appearance. After all, she was only going out with a friend from the past. Richard had disappeared from her life when she had become engaged to Pete and she had never given him another thought.

Impatiently she rubbed dry her newly washed hair and brushed it so that it hung in loose, shining waves down on her shoulders. Then she creamed her face and applied a little make-up. Staring at her reflection, she found herself subconsciously wishing that it was David who was taking her out and realised that he was always in her thoughts. Troubled, she forced herself to banish him from her mind—a difficult task when she recalled him saying that he was in love with her. Surely that couldn't be the case?

His attitude towards her was so strange. He had promised not to bother her again and seemed content to accept the fact that Richard was showing her so much interest. Was he sincere or was it just a ploy to keep her working for him? If that were the case then she had fooled him by resigning. But as she remembered him pleading with her and her half-promise to think again, it made her realise that she could not bear the thought of never seeing him again.

Reluctantly—and with a certain degree of shock—she admitted to herself that she was attracted to him so strongly that it was almost as though she were falling in love with him. Suddenly she shook her head, dismissing what could only be a fantasy. Getting up, she searched through her wardrobe and finally selected a long silk dress which clung to her figure and emphasised her slimness.

Surveying herself in the long mirror, she resolved to make the best of what promised to be a rather boring evening.

To her surprise the evening turned out to be very pleasant. Richard had matured since the early days of their acquaintance and treated her with pleasing deference. He made no secret of his delight that she was no longer engaged to Pete and talked of future dates together, to which she assented cautiously. This renewed friendship could, she realised, turn out to be quite serious if she wanted it to be. But kissing him goodnight, she felt nothing in spite of the suppressed passion she could feel on his part.

Getting ready for bed late that night, she felt a pang of disappointment. It would have been nice if she could have responded to Richard's kiss, and she began to wonder if she was lacking in her capacity to love. With Pete she had never been aroused and had known only relief when they had broken up. Now with Richard she felt only a kind of friendly tolerance. Was there something lacking in her make-up?

She lay awake for a long time, wondering, and finally resolved to take up Richard's invitations and see if she could warm towards him. But before she fell into an uneasy sleep her thoughts reverted to David. Somehow he seemed to be the one man to whom she felt she could respond.

CHAPTER SIX

THE waiting room was full next morning. Rose was kept busy and Susan, too, was fully occupied. A parrot with diarrhoea was prescribed antibiotics in its drinking water, a rabbit's overgrown teeth had to be scaled down and two cats were taken in to be spayed. After making appointments for two other operations, Rose sat down to coffee with a sigh of relief.

'I'll do the pyometra next,' she said. 'I'm afraid it'll be touch and go because she's a very old bitch and overweight into the bargain. Then I'll do the haematoma on that spaniel.' She indicated a young springer spaniel tied up to the wall, who was shaking his head constantly and every now and then whining and growling.

Susan said, 'I'll deal with any emergencies, otherwise I'd like to come and watch.'

Coffee finished, Rose watched while Penny and Wendy made the necessary preparations. After making sure that all instruments had been sterilised, she helped lift the heavy bitch onto the table and gave the anaesthetic injection. As soon as her patient was fully unconscious, Susan came in with Anna to watch. With Wendy operating the anaesthetic machine, Rose shaved the dog's abdomen and made the first incision. Caused by pus in the ovary, the resultant smell was obnoxious but had to be ignored, and Rose worked carefully and methodically.

At last, looking up, she said, 'That's all. I'll stitch her up now. You can turn off the machine, Wendy. She's very deeply under. Let's hope she comes round safely.'

With the dog installed in the warm recovery cage, and Penny watching over her, Rose telephoned the anxious owners and told them of her patient's progress so far. Then she turned her attention to the spaniel with a haematoma. As she waited for the anaesthetic to work, Rose gave a few words of explanation to the nurses. 'A haematoma is when a large swelling appears on the flap of the ear and causes the animal to hang its head towards the same side. The swelling is caused by bruising of the skin, resulting in blood or serum collecting underneath. I'm going to open it up and evacuate the fluid. Then I'll suture the skin in such a way as to prevent any more fluid collecting.'

It was soon dealt with and the ear flap stitched up. Having had a very light anaesthetic, the dog began to come round quickly. With the aid of a protective collar to stop him scratching his ear, he was put in a cage to await his owner that evening. After washing her hands, Rose went into the office while the nurses cleaned up the operating table. To her surprise she found David sitting by the desk. His expression was strange, half uncertain, half grim.

It was a puzzling combination that made her ask, 'Anything wrong?'

'No.' He shook his head, then said impulsively,

'I was just wondering… It's such a lovely day and there's promise of a heat wave so would you like to come out after surgery this evening? Go for a walk over the downs and then a meal—the Downs Hotel is good, I have heard.'

Astonished, Rose stared at him, and as their eyes met she felt a shiver of excitement. Without hesitation she said, 'Yes, I'd like that. I'll leave promptly—Susan can deal with any latecomers, I'm sure. Just give me time to clean up and I'll be with you about seven-thirty.'

He nodded. 'Pete will be on call so I can safely leave any emergencies in his hands—I'm pretty sure he won't play me up again.' He laughed grimly as he went out.

Rose, left to herself, reflected pleasurably on the unexpected invitation. Evening surgery finished on the dot and with half an hour to spare she changed quickly and made some coffee which she took over to the window-seat. Suddenly her attention was caught by the sight of a car pulling up outside. At first she thought it was David, arriving early, but a few seconds showed to her dismay that it was Pete. Now, what on earth did he want? Angrily she went to the door and glared at him.

'Good Lord!' He looked her up and down. 'All dressed up. What's it in aid of?' He pushed past her and indignantly she followed into the room.

'Yes, I'm going out. Very soon. So what do you want?'

His smile was unpleasant. 'Out with David?'

She said nothing but he saw her flush.

'Ah, well, you're playing your cards very cleverly.' He paused. 'Not that it matters to me. I've come to tell you something—in confidence, mind you—and to ask you a favour.' He walked across the room then turned back to face her. 'I'm thinking of leaving here. There's a vacancy in Anna's father's practice and I'm hoping to get the job. What I want to ask is for you to put in a good word for me to Anna. At the moment she's a bit fed up with me because of the trouble the other night when David had to go to that calving. I just want you to stick up for me, praise my work, say I'm very trustworthy and that that incident was a very uncharacteristic slip-up.'

Suddenly he was pleading. 'Please Rose. For old times' sake. I'd really like this job, which would lead to a partnership. I want Anna too. She's a great girl and I think she loves me.'

Rose stared at him. How despicable he was! At last she said, 'Poor Anna.'

He frowned. 'What a stupid thing to say. If I get this job Anna will be happy and so will I.' He paused. 'At the moment she's upset because I let David down, but it won't happen again and you can put things right for me. Now…' He stopped, then went on slowly. 'There's just one more thing. As I said, this is all in confidence. I don't want David to know that I'm thinking of leaving so please keep this to yourself.'

Rose drew a long breath. 'I don't want to enter into a conspiracy with you. You must fight your own battles.'

He frowned. 'Thought you might say that but you should be glad to see me go. It would put an end to David's suspicions that you and I are in league against him.'

Rose was silent. So he knew that David was uneasy about her relationship with Pete. It certainly would be a good thing if he left—it would save her constantly having to deny that there was anything hidden from him. At last she said slowly, 'Well, I wish you luck. But I don't want to be bound by a promise of secrecy. I might have to tell him if he asks me.'

'No! You can't do that!' Pete's anger was reflected in his eyes. They glowered at her and she took a step back in momentary alarm. 'After all, I might not get the job and that would put paid to my prospects here.' He paused. 'I almost wish I hadn't told you. Please, Rose—for old times' sake.'

Rose weakened. After all, it was hardly likely that David would ask her. 'Oh, all right,' she said deliberately, 'but you will give him plenty of notice, won't you?'

'Of course I will. And will you intercede with Anna for me?'

'No. Anna must make up her own mind,' she said firmly.

He shook his head regretfully. 'Well, I suppose I'll have to accept that. It was the whole point of my visit to you. I just have to hope that you will keep your word and not let anything out to David.'

There was a sound outside and Rose went hurriedly to the window, then turned agitatedly to Pete.

'It's David! Oh, dear, now I shall have to explain why you are here.'

Pete turned to leave. 'Tell him I came to apologise for having dragged you out the other night. I hear you went with him.'

He closed the door behind him, leaving Rose in complete turmoil. David would never believe such a feeble excuse but she couldn't think of anything better. How she resented Pete for trapping her into yet another deception.

She watched from the window as the two men met. Then Pete got into his car, waved his hand and then drove away, while David stood, looking after him, as though in deep thought. With a shrug of his shoulders he came towards her door. Dashing into the kitchen, Rose put on the kettle. She would make a coffee to greet him while she tried to think of a good reason for Pete's visit, but as she waited her mind was blank. Finally she went to the door to greet him smilingly, only to be met with a deep frown.

'What was Pete doing here?' His voice was harsh as he came into the room and her heart sank.

She turned into the kitchen to see to the coffee, and over her shoulder she said lightly, 'He'd heard that I went with you to that calving and came to apologise for, as he said, dragging me out.'

'Hmm.' David waited while she poured the coffee and began to drink it standing up. She indicated a chair but he shook his head and stood, looking at her searchingly. 'That seems a bit unnecessary. He didn't show any remorse when I spoke to him this morning, even though I told him if he let me down again that would be the end of any prospects of a partnership. Did he mention that to you?'

'No.' She shook her head. 'He wasn't here very long.'

'Does he come here often?'

'No,' she said again, but could feel her colour rising and hurriedly gulped down her coffee. It was very hot and she was so tense that she choked. Embarrassed, she turned away from his penetrating gaze and went over to the window, putting the coffee down on the side table. Suddenly she felt him strike her smartly on the back but she waved him away, gasping.

'It's all right. The coffee was too hot.' Gradually she managed to control her breathing but her voice was strained as she said, 'I'll get a jacket. We'd better go.'

'Yes,' he said coolly, and his attitude remained distant as he followed her towards the car. Holding the door, he said, 'I thought we'd drive out onto the downs then walk from there. Is that OK?'

She nodded, hoping he was satisfied with her explanation but worried by his lack of friendliness. He was suspicious, of that she felt sure, but there was nothing she could do about it. She began to talk lightly, enthusing about the evening, and gradually to her relief he seemed to relax.

It was indeed a beautiful evening and when David had parked the car up onto the downs he came round to open her door. 'Let's get away from these people.' He indicated a group standing on the cliff edge, looking down at the sea.

She nodded. 'They don't look as though they're going to walk very far.'

They soon left them behind and once they were out of sight they strolled along in silence. Suddenly he took her hand, swung it in unison with his and drew a long, deep breath.

'It's wonderful up here, isn't it?' he asked, glancing at her glowing face. 'A beautiful evening with a beautiful girl.'

The feel of her hand held so tightly in his made her heart beat faster but she tried to tell herself that it meant nothing.

'You're very quiet.' His voice broke in on her thoughts and she flushed almost guiltily. 'Is something worrying you?'

'No,' she said hastily. 'I'm just enjoying the silence up here. Only the sound of the gulls. See how they fly about the cliffs below us.' She withdrew her hand, walked towards the edge and looked down.

'Careful.' He followed her. 'You said you hadn't much of a head for heights and these cliffs seem to draw one.'

She continued to gaze down, then suddenly exclaimed, 'Look. There's something down on the beach—it looks like an animal.'

He came forward and followed her pointing finger. 'God! Yes, it is. A dog, I think. The poor thing must have been chasing a rabbit or something. It looks dead but I'd better go and see.'

'You can't climb down, it's impossible.' Rose turned to face him and he saw her alarm.

'No, of course. But we're fairly near that cliff pass I told you about.'

When at last they came to the opening he said, 'I'll go and see if I can carry it up here. You stay here.'

Disregarding her nervousness, he left her for what was only a short time, but to her it seemed an eternity before he landed on the beach. Then she saw him bend down and examine the animal, and her fears grew. The examination didn't take long and he rose to his feet and stood, looking down at the dog. Suddenly coming to a decision, he bent down again, lifted the body into his arms and began the long trek back along the beach and up the steep path. Rose watched him fearfully and saw that there was no sign of life from his heavy burden. When David finally reached her he put it down and stood for a while in silence. Bending down, Rose saw that it was lifeless.

'It died just as I reached it,' David said. 'Poor thing.' He paused. 'The name and address of the owner is attached to its collar. He's a farmer—I know him. Jim Roberts. Lives a couple of miles inland. We had better take the dog back—can't just leave it here. They must have been worrying about it—at least they'll now know what happened to it.'

Rose watched as he lifted the heavy dog once more and began to walk back towards the car. As she watched the gentle way David put his burden into the boot of his car her sadness turned to admiration. He was putting himself in the owner's place, visualising the anxiety and trying to save more worry.

Nevertheless she said gently, 'You could have taken the collar off and given it to the farmer.'

He looked at her seriously as he held the car door open. 'Yes, I suppose I could. But if it were my dog I would want it back.' He paused. 'So you think I'm being foolish, do you?'

'No,' she said slowly, 'not when you put it like that. You are being very kind.'

His expression lightened. 'Thank you, Rose. Let's go to the farm and get it over.'

The farmhouse stood back from the main road, and as they pulled up in the yard opposite the back door Rose said, 'I'll stay in the car.' As soon as David pulled the bell the door opened and a middle-aged man greeted David after a moment's hesitation.

Turning, he spoke to his wife and she came out and listened while David told the sad story. She burst into tears, then followed the men round to the back of the car. As Mr Roberts gathered his dog into his arms Mrs Roberts beckoned to Rose to follow them into the kitchen, where her husband laid his burden on a large dog bed in an alcove, then produced some glasses.

'You deserve a drink for bringing Jasper back. We wouldn't have wanted him washed out to sea.'

After covering the dog with a blanket he poured out the drinks and his wife dried her eyes and said sadly, 'We haven't had Jasper long but this isn't the first time he has gone missing. He had lived with an old man in a cottage on the downs and he had this craving to run wild and chase rabbits. I suppose it was inevitable that he would meet this kind of fate.'

She paused as the door opened. 'Ah! here's Judy.'

A tall, slim girl with blonde shoulder-length hair stood still for a moment, looking down at the covered dog. Then she said quietly, 'It's all right. I saw you bring Jasper in and I guessed what had happened. It was kind of you to bring him back. Did you do it for old times' sake?'

Going up to David, she put an arm round him and looked up at him smilingly. He stiffened slightly and patted her rather awkwardly on the shoulder.

'Well, when I saw your name on his collar I couldn't leave him on the beach.'

She sighed. 'It's a long time since we walked on the downs together, isn't it?'

Mr Roberts coughed. 'Have a drink, Judy. It'll help you pull yourself together.'

She took the glass he handed her and turned to Rose. 'David and I were great friends once. It seems like fate that we should meet again like this.' Then her face hardened as she studied Rose carefully. 'So you were walking over the downs with him. I suppose you have taken my place.'

Embarrassed by this open hostility, Rose was speechless.

David said hurriedly, turning to Mrs Roberts, 'We must go now. Thank you for the drink. I'm sorry about Jasper.'

Mrs Roberts's eyes were on her daughter, looking at her apprehensively as though expecting another tactless outburst, but Judy stood still, staring at David almost beseechingly. As he turned away she went up to him.

'A kiss?' she said softly, 'For old times' sake?'

Rose moved away, pretending not to hear, but she saw David bend his head obediently and give her a quick peck on the cheek.

As they went through the door Judith said in a normal voice, 'I'll look you up in your surgery one of these days.'

Driving to the Downs Hotel at last Rose said quietly, 'Judy didn't seem very upset at Jasper's death, did she?'

'No,' David said curtly, then, after a moment's pause, 'She doesn't care for animals at all. That was the reason why—' He stopped and she saw his hands tighten on the steering-wheel, but he said no more, leaving Rose consumed with curiosity. Obviously he had no wish to confide in her so she did her best to keep the conversation light throughout the meal. Gradually his tension lessened until at last, as they were drinking their coffee, he put down his cup and sighed.

'Well, I suppose you've guessed that Judy and I had an affair some time ago. I was a fool—taken in by her from the start. What finished me was her dislike of animals, which at first she had concealed.

'It all came to a head one day when we were out in the car and came across a dog lying by the side of the road. Naturally I got out and went to see if it was still alive. I insisted on taking it back to the surgery. We had been on our way to visit some friends and she was furious when I rang to put them off, saying I had to attend to the dog. Actually, I managed to save it but Judy said I should have left it to die, saying what did it matter if there was one dog more or less? That completely finished it for me.'

Suddenly Rose realised that her heart had lightened and a bewildering knot in her stomach had relaxed. Judith and David—an affair which David had ended but which Judith seemed to want to renew. How much had it cost him to break off the relationship? He had plainly been moved by her unexpected arrival.

Impulsively, she asked, 'Did you care for her very much?' She immediately regretted her question when she heard him draw a sharp breath.

He said curtly, 'I was in love with her.'

Rose felt rebuffed and said no more, but after a few moments of silence he added quietly, 'At least I thought I was, but I now know it was an illusion. Sometimes I think that love is always an illusion and can be conquered by the discovery of some grave fault in the object of one's desire.' He picked up his coffee, gulped it down and then looked at his watch. 'I suppose we ought to be getting back.'

Rose sat deep in thought as they drove along, and the memory of his last sentence echoed in her mind. Was he referring to her and his suspicions that she was hiding something from him? He said he loved her but maybe he was becoming disillusioned again. It would account for his seeming indifference to the fact that Richard was showing such interest in her and his probing questions were merely confirming his conviction that he was being deceived. Deception on her part would be a 'grave fault', therefore killing all thoughts of love.

Well, she thought rebelliously, if he could turn love off and on like that, it couldn't possibly be the real thing. She herself knew that if she loved someone she would overlook his faults and love him just the same. The thought hardened her attitude towards him, making her feel cool and rather distant. On arrival at her cottage he stood in her doorway, obviously waiting to be asked in, and for a moment she felt inclined to rebuff him. Seeing her hesitation, he turned away but instantly she regretted her discourtesy.

She said, 'Would you like to come in for a nightcap?' Then she stood back to let him in, adding, 'Thank you for a lovely evening. I enjoyed it very much.'

'I'm glad,' he said simply, 'though I had the feeling that you were a bit bored.'

He followed her into the kitchen and sat down at the table, watching her put on the kettle and spoon coffee into cups.

She said quietly, 'You never bore me, though sometimes I don't understand you.'

He laughed shortly. 'That makes two of us. I find it difficult to understand you.' He paused. 'There seems to be some kind of barrier between us—a barrier I would very much like to pull down.'

She turned back to the boiling kettle and her heart beat faster as she made the coffee but she said nothing. How could she explain the web of deceit in which she felt herself entangled? She put the coffee on the table and smiled at him gently.

Gazing at her searchingly, he sighed. 'Well, I suppose I must leave things as they are and just hope that some time or other the barrier will come down of its own accord. Perhaps it's my imagination and you are all you appear to be.' He paused. 'Let's change the conversation. How do you feel about Richard?'

The unexpected question made her flush but she answered frankly, 'No particular feeling. He's just a friend.'

'He'd like to be more.' David's tone was verging on the sarcastic. 'I feel almost sorry for him.'

'Don't waste your pity,' Rose said sharply. 'I'm sure he'll get over my lack of response. I'm absolutely heart-free.'

'Well, I'm not. Perhaps I should pity myself.' His reply disconcerted her but purposely she pretended to misunderstand him.

'I suppose you regret having broken up with Judith Roberts. She seems to want to take up with you again but you are too much of a perfectionist to overlook her dislike of animals—her grave fault.'

'Good God! So you think I'm a perfectionist, do you?'

'Yes,' she said defiantly. 'One fault in her character and you drop her like a stone.'

He flushed. 'That wasn't the only reason. You shouldn't condemn me out of hand like that.'

'Well, I can only go by what you've told me.'

Suddenly she lost interest and put her hand up as though to finish the conversation. She said coolly, 'In any case, it's nothing to do with me.' She changed the subject. 'More coffee?'

'No, thanks.' He frowned. 'I must be going.' He stood up and as she also rose he added, 'This good weather looks like lasting. How about coming for a swim one evening this week?'

She was about to shake her head but suddenly the idea was appealing. She said slowly, 'That would be nice but I don't want to go where we found the dog. I don't like the idea of going down that steep path. I told you, I haven't got a good head for heights.'

'OK. If we go in the evening the main beach won't be crowded. Shall we say tomorrow? Susan can look after the surgery and I'll leave any farm calls to Pete.'

'Not tomorrow. It's Susan's day off.'

'Day after, then?'

She nodded and as he went towards the door she said laughingly, 'I'm not a wonderful swimmer.'

He smiled. 'I'll look after you.' Suddenly he put his arm round her and turned her towards him. Face to face she waited for his kiss, and when it came she made no resistance. At first he kissed her gently, then his arm tightened and his mouth searched hers fiercely. Alarmed, she stiffened and began to struggle. Immediately he released her and said grimly, 'I'm sorry. Was that too much for you?'

She looked at him reproachfully. 'You said you wouldn't bother me any more.'

His face was pale and a muscle twitched in his temple.

'Did I? Well, all I can say is that you are irresistible.' He went through the open door. 'Don't forget. The day after tomorrow.'

Speechless, she watched him drive away. Going back into the kitchen, she poured herself another coffee. Her mind was in turmoil and although she tried to calm her breathing she couldn't stop the rapid beating of her heart. The feel of his arms gripping her so fiercely and his mouth on hers in that desperate and demanding kiss left her trembling in a way that was entirely new to her. Surely, she thought, she wasn't in love with him. That would be disastrous in view of all that she had hidden from him.

Gradually she calmed down and resolved to keep him at a safe distance and try and quell the emotions he had stirred in her. Perhaps she ought not to go swimming with him—it might be too dangerous and lead to another scene. She sighed. Better sleep on it and see how she felt in the morning.

But morning surgery gave her no time for reflection. Susan's day off and a waiting room full of clients kept her fully occupied, and with several operations to do she only had time for a quick coffee.

'I'll do that dog with an ulcer in its eye first,' she told the nurses, 'then I must take some skin scrapings from the dog with skin trouble. I'm pretty sure it's mange, but I must check to be sure. Then there are three rats to be castrated.' Rose laughed. 'All the

same, I can't imagine why anyone should breed rats.
I suppose there must be a demand for them.'

'Why does the breeder want them castrated?'

'They are going to be sold as pets.' Rose got up
then, pausing by the window, she stopped. 'Someone's coming. Must be an emergency.'

She watched as a girl got out of the car, carrying
a cat basket. She stiffened as recognition came.
Judith Roberts. Well, she had promised to look
David up and she hadn't wasted much time. But he
had gone to a horse with colic and there was no
knowing when he would be back so Judith was going to be unlucky. Rose turned to the nurses and
warned them to put their coffee away. The table was
cleared by the time Judith Roberts came in.

'I know it's past surgery time,' she said brightly,
'but I had a job to find this cat. My mother is anxious about her. She's been off colour for a while.'
She deposited the basket on the table and looked
around. 'Is David here? I'd like him to look her
over.'

Rose said, 'Well, it's my job really. I and a colleague do all the small animal work. David is out,
seeing a horse with colic.'

Judith's face fell. 'Oh, that's a pity. Well, I suppose you will have to see this wretched animal, then.
I don't suppose there's much wrong with it.'

Opening the cage door, Rose saw a young tabby
cat, which gazed fiercely at her and looked remark-
ably healthy. Its tail waved angrily as she drew it
out and held it firmly. Wendy handed over the thermometer and Rose inserted it, much to the cat's in-

dignation, but she managed to keep it in place. Then suddenly it twisted away with its claws out, but Rose was ready for it and, speaking soothingly, she managed to calm it down.

Suddenly Judith hit the cat across its face and, ignoring the gasp from Wendy, said angrily, 'Horrid thing. I can't think why my mother makes a pet of her. She's almost wild, anyway.'

'There was no need for that,' Rose said sharply. 'The poor little thing is only acting instinctively. Actually…' She drew the thermometer out and studied it carefully. 'Temperature is normal. What did you say was the matter with her?'

Judith hesitated. 'Well, my mother asked me to have her examined to make sure she's OK.'

Rose took the towel offered by Wendy, wrapped it tightly round the resisting cat and proceeded to examine it, looking in its mouth and ears and gradually moving the towel so that she could feel it all over. Then she listened to its heart and searched for any trouble. As she had suspected, it had all been an excuse for Judith to renew her acquaintance with David. She was just going to put the cat back in its traveling basket when David himself walked in. She saw his face freeze when he saw Judith who, ignoring his lack of welcome, smiled at him beguilingly.

'I never thought I would be seeing you so soon but as this poor little thing…' she indicated the imprisoned cat, mewing indignantly '…was a bit off colour and as she is so special to me I've brought her in for an examination. Apparently, she's all right.' She shot a malicious glance at Rose. 'But

perhaps you would take a look at her to make sure.'
She looked at him appealingly. 'I'm so fond of her.'

'Good Lord!' David looked incredulous. 'I
thought you disliked animals. You've changed a bit,
haven't you?'

'Oh, yes, I find it so unbearable to see them suffer. Will you just examine Tibby, please? Just to
reassure me.'

Rose, trying not to show her disgust at the act
Judith was putting on, prepared to open the cage
door.

David said sharply, 'No. There's absolutely no
need. Rose is the small animal vet here and her ver-
dict is all that is necessary.' He paused. 'I'll say
goodbye now. I have work to do.' He went towards
the office but Judith followed him in.

As she shut the door Rose heard her say, 'My
father would like you to do our veterinary work so
could you come over on Sunday for a drink and
discuss it?'

Rose heard no more but her eyes met Wendy's
who shook her head in disgust. 'Let's hope David
doesn't fall for her little game,' she said. 'It's so
obvious anyone could see through it.'

But it appeared David had been taken in because,
ushering her out a few minutes later, he seemed
quite friendly. He said goodbye, adding, 'I'll try and
make it on Sunday.' Then he went silently back into
the office.

Rose was finishing off an operation when he came
out and stood silently watching while she sutured up

the wound, having taken out a large tumour from a cat.

As she snipped off the thread he said, 'I'd like you to come with me on Sunday to the Robertses' farm. If I agree to do work there it would be a good idea if you came along too.'

She looked at him doubtfully. 'I don't see—'

'Well, of course,' he said impatiently, 'if I'm not available you would have to go.'

'But Pete—'

'I'm talking about an emergency when neither Pete nor I are available.'

'Surely that's not very likely and in any case I'm not invited.'

'Never mind that.' His voice was sharp. 'Make your arrangements with Susan, please.' He paused. 'I'm off now to deal with a mastitis case at Hill Farm. See you later.'

Rose handed the cat over to Penny, and Wendy, who had been in charge of the anaesthetic machine, said thoughtfully, 'That was a pretty feeble excuse, wasn't it? It sounds as though he needs your protection.'

'It's absurd.' Rose paused, then said slowly, 'I think I'll suggest that Pete should go instead.' She pondered for a few moments, before saying half to herself, 'I'll settle it with David when we go swimming tomorrow evening.' No sooner had she spoken than she regretted it for Wendy smiled broadly.

'Well, well,' she said with a hint of mockery in her voice, 'let's hope it keeps fine for you. Things are progressing.'

Rose felt her colour rising. 'What's wrong with going for an evening swim?' But as she had asked the question she knew what the nurses would make of it. Looked at from their point of view, it did seem as though there was something going on between herself and David.

'Nothing wrong with it at all,' Wendy said smoothly. 'I just hope you will have a good time and be able to persuade David to take Pete to the Robertses', instead of dragging you along.'

CHAPTER SEVEN

NEXT day after busy surgeries Rose felt hot and tired. The prospect of an evening swim was appealing, though she felt she would rather have gone alone. However, there was no getting out of it, and when David arrived to pick her up she was ready and waiting.

The sea was calm and the tide was going out when they reached the beach, which at this time of day was almost empty. David parked on the grassy space reserved for cars and Rose slipped out of her loose white dress. She stood up in her flattering blue and white swimsuit and waited while David shed his trousers to reveal his swimming trunks. He reached into the back of the car and pulled out a large beach towel, then cast her an admiring look as his gaze swept over her as they walked down towards the water.

They stood for a few moments, looking at each other, but he didn't move any closer. Then he said, 'Race you.' He plunged in headlong. Without thinking, she followed and began swimming straight out in an endeavour to catch him up. He was a strong swimmer and was a long way ahead and eventually she began to tire. Turning on her back, she floated for a few minutes then resolved to go back. It was then that she became aware of the pull of the outgoing tide. The beach seemed a long way off and she reproached herself for having ventured out so far. Struggling on, she found she was fighting a losing battle as with every stroke she made the sea just pulled her back again.

Gasping and frightened, she looked back and saw David floating in a leisurely fashion. Although she trod water and waved frantically, he didn't seem to notice. Wondering how long she could keep afloat, she called to him but still there was no response. She called again and again until her voice cracked and she started choking. At last he looked up saw her distress and began to swim furiously towards her.

As he drew near she tried to explain but he said firmly, 'Turn on your back.' He towed her until they reached the shallow water and she was able to stand.

He stood beside her with his arm still round her and she gasped, 'Oh, thank you, thank you.'

'Why on earth did you go out so far?' His voice was full of concern.

She said shamefacedly, 'Well, I tried to catch you up.'

His eyebrows rose and he said, 'I'll get the towel.' Turning, he sped up the beach, leaving her to walk slowly out of the water. Enveloping her in the large beach towel, he stood with his arm around her. Then he drew her slowly down to sit on the pebbled ridge and said, 'As soon as you're ready we'll get back into the car,' adding with a frown, 'Of all the stupid things to do.'

She stiffened, resenting his criticism, and said sharply, 'I told you I wasn't much of a swimmer.'

'You don't say!' His sarcasm stung and drove away any feelings of gratitude.

'Well, I did say, and you said you would look after me. I don't think swimming off into the distance, without waiting to see how I was managing or even glancing in my direction occasionally, was exactly looking after me.'

'You're right,' he said, suddenly repentant. 'I had completely forgotten what you had said in the excitement of thinking we were racing one another. I'm very sorry.' He paused and added gently, 'Are you ready to come back to the car?' Bending down, he made to help her up. As she accepted his arm she caught a glimpse of a familiar figure, coming along the beach towards them. At her exclamation David turned. 'Good God! It's Richard! What on earth is he doing here?'

He told them as soon as they were within earshot. 'Lucky I found you. I went to the surgery on the off chance of seeing you, Rose. They told me that you had gone for a swim so I came to look for you.' He paused and glanced at David. 'I didn't realize you weren't alone.'

Rose felt embarrassed as she caught sight of David's face. Obviously resentful at this intrusion, he was frowning. His voice was cold as he said, 'We're just going to the car. Rose has had enough.'

'Not too tired to come out with me for a drink, I hope,' Richard said cheerfully, ignoring the lack of welcome in David's voice.

Rose, still smarting from David's thoughtlessness, forgot her resolve to finish with Richard and said brightly, 'I'd like that, but first I must get dressed and tidied up. My things are in David's car so you can follow us back and have some coffee while I get ready.'

David's silence was oppressive as they walked back to the car, but Richard seemed not to notice or chose to ignore the atmosphere. His own car was parked alongside David's and as Richard got in he said, 'You go ahead. I'll follow.'

Once inside David's car Rose discarded the beach towel and slipped on her dress, while David pulled on his shirt and trousers, still without saying a word. He waited until Rose was ready, then slipped the car into gear and moved onto the road. At last he spoke.

'As you seem to have ditched me, I'll go as soon as I've dropped you off at your cottage.'

Already Rose was regretting her rash acceptance of Richard's invitation, but it was too late to do anything about it so she nodded in agreement and the rest of the journey passed in cold silence. On their arrival David waited while she let herself into the cottage, then drove off at speed, his face grim with anger. A few minutes later Richard arrived and stood watching as she made coffee, before going to tidy herself. As she handed him a mug he laughed.

'David wasn't best pleased when you agreed to come out with me, was he? I hope I haven't broken up any prior engagement you had with him.'

'We hadn't planned anything. Anyway, I'm a bit

tired so I won't want to be late back. Just a drink with you, that's all.'

Ignoring Richard's obvious disappointment, she went to her bedroom and tried to conquer the depression which threatened to overwhelm her. Why, she asked herself as she ran a quick shower, had she been so rude as to snub David so openly and why had she let herself in for a date with Richard when he meant nothing to her? She could have wept with frustration but knew she must try and make the best of it. Maybe she could make it up with David tomorrow, though how she could accomplish this she had no idea.

Twenty minutes later she went downstairs, drank a quick coffee and went out to Richard's car. He seemed a bit subdued at first but cheered up when, at her suggestion, they pulled up outside a pretty country pub. Seated at a table in a corner, she refused his offer of food and waited while he went to the bar to get the drinks. A few minutes later, seated opposite her, he began to talk earnestly.

'I've found a village where I can settle down with a new practice. It's some way from here and it's just what I want as it's got great potential. So now I'm going to ask you if you would join me and help build it up. Now, don't shake your head like that, Rose. I haven't finished. Actually, I've put things in the wrong order. What I would really like would be for you to marry me. I'm sure we could be very happy together. Will you please think it over? Please, Rose. I'm very much in love with you.'

Rose was stunned. Too stunned to find words in

which to refuse him, and her hesitation seemed to encourage him. He reached out, took her hand and said again, 'Please, Rose.'

Slowly she shook her head. Drawing a long breath, she found her voice. 'I'm sorry, Richard, but it's no to both your questions. I don't love you. I like you as a friend but that's all, and I'm sure we wouldn't be happy together. As for helping you build up your practice, it would be too difficult, with you feeling for me as you do.' She withdrew her hand, saw he was about to protest and shook her head again. 'I'm glad you've found somewhere and I wish you all the luck in the world.'

'Oh, Rose!' He looked so downcast that her heart was wrung. She hated having to refuse him but it had to be done. She finished her drink hurriedly, waited till his glass was empty and rose to her feet. 'I must go back now,' she said. 'I don't want to be late. I've got a difficult op to do tomorrow.'

Wordlessly he followed her out to the car. As he held the door open for her, he said sorrowfully, 'Well, let's keep in touch. If by any chance you should change your mind and decide to leave your present job…' He paused. 'I suppose you're in love with David. That's what is keeping you there.'

She flushed quickly but her denial was firm. 'No, you're wrong there. I'm not in love with anyone.'

Her last words echoed in her head when, having said goodbye to Richard, she sat in her kitchen, drinking coffee. They didn't ring true. She was not heart-free. More and more, thoughts of David flooded her mind. Briefly she wondered what her answer would have been if, instead of Richard, it had been David who had asked her to marry him. The mere idea caused her heart to beat fast but, not willing to face up to her question, she hurriedly finished her coffee and began to get ready for bed.

Next morning she had a busy surgery. Most of the cases were fairly run of the mill but a cat with diarrhoea presented a problem. She diagnosed inflammatory bowel disease, judging from the fact that the cat was vomiting and suffering from weight loss and now diarrhoea was occurring. After her examination Rose decided the cat must be hospitalised in order to run various tests.

The owners, however, were reluctant to leave their pet and insisted that it be treated at home. However much Rose tried to convince them, they were adamant and finally she had to compromise. She prescribed a balanced prescription diet with no other food allowed for a period of four weeks. Along with the diet she prescribed prednisolone twice daily for at least four weeks. After telling them that the cat must be confined, she knew that was all she could do.

When they had gone she scrubbed up and got ready to do an entropion operation on a young puppy. It was a delicate operation and Susan came in to watch.

Explaining what the operation involved, Rose said, 'As you can see, his eye is half-closed and the lower lid is turned inwards so that the eyelashes are in direct contact with the eye. It's a question of plastic surgery. I shall take a piece of skin the shape of a half-moon from below the eyelid, draw the skin together, pull the eyelid down and stitch on the skin graft. In about ten days I'll take the stitches out and the puppy will have a normal eye.'

It all went exactly as she had said, though when she was cutting out the half-moon of skin she warned her audience, 'This is the tricky bit. If I take too little it won't pull the eyelid down enough.'

Susan said nervously, 'I think you're just saying that to make me apprehensive.'

Rose shook her head. 'No. It's just to remind me to be careful. It is very easy to be complacent with operations and that's when mistakes occur.'

When it was over Susan said, 'I've not actually come across this condition as yet but now I feel as though I would be able to cope. I'm so glad you are here. It was a very good idea of David's that you should give me the benefit of your experience. We're very well staffed here, aren't we?' She paused. 'Talking of which, has Anna told you that she wants this weekend off?'

Rose murmured something vague and, making some excuse, she went into the office to collect her thoughts. If Anna had decided to have this weekend off, it must be that Pete would be doing the same and once more she would have to pretend that she knew nothing about it. If only she hadn't promised him to keep it a secret. It all added to the burden of deceit that made things so awkward for her with David. As though in answer to her thoughts, she heard his voice in the outer room and her heart gave a leap as the door opened and he came into the office.

He looked annoyed and said abruptly, 'Pete wants this coming weekend off and apparently so does Anna. Has he spoken to you about it?'

'Well she's due for a weekend, isn't she?' Rose said as calmly as she could.

He still looked irritated and said sharply, 'Yes, I suppose so, but it's a coincidence that Pete wants the same time off, isn't it? Did you know anything about it?'

Here it was—the direct question that Rose had dreaded. She half turned away from his searching gaze. Her face must have betrayed her for he said sharply, 'You're hiding something again. You did know. Good grief! Why do you have to be so secretive with me? When did he tell you? Was it when he visited you the other evening?'

She nodded miserably. 'Yes, he bound me to secrecy.'

'And you agreed?' he said explosively. 'What possessed you? What right has he to make such a condition? And why did he want it to be a secret?'

'So many questions,' Rose said resentfully. 'What does it matter anyway? You know now.'

'There's more to it than meets the eye,' he said frowningly. 'I believe they're going together to see her father—he's a vet, isn't he? That's it.' He nodded to himself. 'Pete is hoping to get a job with him. Well, I don't mind. We have never really got on together. So no partnership.' He stopped, walked over to the window and stood, looking out onto the car park, deep in thought. Then he turned to Rose, who was just on the point of leaving the room. He said, 'Don't go. Just tell me what it will mean to you if Pete leaves.'

'Absolutely nothing,' Rose said vehemently, 'in fact, like you, I shall be glad. Though I'm sorry for Anna—she's in love with him.'

'Foolish girl! But are you sure it's pity you feel for her? Isn't it more like, well, envy perhaps?'

'Oh! Good grief!' Rose shook her head vigorously. 'Why do you persist in this farcical notion that I still care for Pete? What evidence do you have? I assure you—'

He took her up quickly. '"Care for" is just what I mean. You kept his confidence when there was no need, you express regret that Anna is in love with him—all along you seem to defend him. I am sorry but it appears to me that you do still care for him.'

Utterly bewildered by his reasoning, and haunted by the memory of having deceived him in the past, Rose could stand no more. Tears welled up in her eyes and she turned away to hide them, but he had seen how troubled she was.

He said more gently, 'Rose, I don't want to hurt you. The truth is, I long for you to be open with me but you have put up this confounded defensive wall between us...'

'If only...' Her voice was choked. 'If only you would believe me.'

He said nothing but stood staring at her, as though trying to read her mind. At last he said, 'What I don't understand is why he told you that he was taking the weekend off with Anna and then bound you to secrecy. It seems pointless.'

Rose hesitated, then suddenly decided to break her enforced promise to Pete. After all, he was the cause of the web of deceit in which she was caught. Why should she get further enmeshed? She said slowly, 'He wanted me to put in a good word on his behalf to Anna. To praise him up to her. She was, it seemed, becoming disillusioned with him. When I refused he bound me to secrecy with regard to you in case he didn't succeed in landing a job with her father.'

'Ah!' David drew a long breath. 'So that was it.' He paused. 'He seems to have you under his thumb. And you wouldn't praise him to Anna?' He stopped and frowned. 'Obviously you didn't want Anna to make it up with him. Why not?' He answered his own question. 'Because you are still in love with him. That was it, wasn't it?'

'Oh, David!' Rose looked at him despairingly. 'Why do you always misinterpret everything? It's no use. Even when I tell you the truth, you twist it round to make me out to being deceitful. I give up. No wonder—' She stopped, remembering the time when she really had been deceitful. She said again, 'It's no use.' She moved away.

He made no attempt to follow and she left him in the office, staring after her.

For the rest of the day they saw very little of each other. Rose was kept occupied with very busy surgeries and David had a lot of farm work. The hot weather brought the usual cases of skin troubles, fleas and digestive upsets. One client brought in a spaniel which she wanted Rose to examine.

She said, 'I don't understand it. She had her season three months ago but she seems to be pregnant. She keeps whining, collects all her toys together and makes a nest for them in all kinds of strange places. She keeps scratching up the carpets and seems uneasy all the time.'

Rose smiled. 'I think I know what it is. She has never been spayed, has she?'

'No. I don't believe in spaying. I think Nature should take its course.'

'Well…' Rose began her examination, then nodded as she recognised the signs. She said, 'This is what's known as a false or phantom pregnancy. It often happens to unspayed bitches.' She laughed. 'It can happen to humans too. It is a bit of a nuisance, but it only lasts for about two to three weeks. Sometimes an injection can be given but I'm not in favour of treating it medically. It is best left, as you say, to Nature to take its course.' She stroked her patient gently and smiled down at her. 'You can't help it, can you?'

Turning to her client, she said, 'Would you consider having her spayed when this is over? It would put an end to this condition, which may well happen again.'

The owner shook her head. 'No. I'll put up with it now that I now what it is.' She paused. 'Well, that's what I think now but perhaps if it happens again I may change my mind. I'll let you know if I do.'

'Well, the best time for a spay is midway between seasons,' said Rose as she handed the spaniel over.

As soon as she had gone Wendy said, 'I can't understand why some people are against having bitches spayed unless, of course, they want to breed from them. But I suppose it's a question of fear— they don't realise what a simple operation it is.'

'Fear is a strange emotion.' David had come into the surgery. 'It makes people do things out of character.' He had been looking at Rose as he had spoken, and her heart jumped.

Had his remark been meant for her? She moved away from the examination table and went to wash her hands while the nurses prepared coffee.

'How's your entropion patient?' he asked.

She replied, 'Fine. He went home this morning. Stitches out in ten days.'

He nodded approvingly then said, 'Come into the office for a moment, will you, Rose?' Turning to the nurses, he said, 'Back in a moment for coffee.'

Reluctantly she followed him. Once in his office he shut the door and stood for a moment as if undecided. Finally he said, 'I've an appointment with Mr Trent about buying his practice. I'd like you to come with me. The appointment is tomorrow afternoon at three o'clock. I'll come for you at two-thirty. OK?'

Rose wanted to refuse, wanted to say that her presence would be unnecessary, but somehow the words wouldn't come. She nodded slowly and he departed, leaving her angry with herself. He was taking it for granted that she would be staying in his employ. Finally she shrugged to herself. What did it matter after all? There was so much between the actual acquisition of the practice, signing of contracts, fitting it all up—anything could happen between now and then.

Although David seemed to think she was capable of running a small practice, she didn't really know if she wanted the job. It would mean a complete change of environment and a rather lonely situation. Of course, she would be a partner but, weighing it up, she didn't think it was worth it. However, he wanted her to go with him and probably give her opinion so she would try and keep an open mind.

She was ready and waiting when he picked her up at two-thirty next day, and as they drove along he talked of the practice they were going to see.

'I'm rather nervous of taking this on,' he said. 'It's a big outlay but I feel I must in order to keep the opposition at bay. It's only ten miles away and if another vet takes it over it could make a big difference to me. I spoke to Mr Trent yesterday and it appears that several people are interested. Thank goodness I have first refusal, but I have to make up my mind quickly because the old boy is anxious to move on.'

Rose, surprised to hear him expressing doubt, began to feel interested. She saw his point about the prospect of future opposition but said consolingly, 'I don't think you have much fear from another vet. Your practice is flourishing and there's surely room for two in this area. Has Mr Trent got a mixed practice or is it only for small animals?'

'Oh, he only does small animals, but a new man might well want to take on some farm work.'

'Well, farmers don't change vets easily, and you already have as many as you can cope with.'

He nodded, as though in agreement. Encouraged, she went on, 'Of course, you could let Richard take it on. Being a friend, you might come to an agreement whereby he didn't encroach on your territory.'

'I don't think that would work,' he said quickly. 'I couldn't make any conditions. I wouldn't have the right.'

He subsided into silence but she could see from the occasional glance at his face that he was considering her argument. Suddenly he said, 'How would you feel if I turned it down? After all, I promised you that you could run it by yourself. Would you be disappointed?'

She hesitated, wondering if she could tell him that she was having second thoughts. She evaded the question by saying, 'You've taken for granted that I shall be staying with you.'

'Well, you said—'

'I never promised anything. I said I would think it over.'

'I distinctly got the impression that when I offered you a partnership and the branch practice you were quite keen on the idea. Anyway, you haven't answered my question. Would you be disappointed if I turned it down?' He paused then added hastily, 'You would still have the partnership, of course.'

Once more she tried to avoid the question and said slowly, 'I would like a partnership very much.'

'But what about the branch practice?' he persisted. 'How do you feel about that?'

Forced to answer, she said slowly, 'I'm a bit doubtful. I know it would be a great opportunity for me but—' She stopped, unable to tell him that she didn't want to be isolated and would miss seeing him as often as she did now.

'But what?' He glanced sideways at her. 'You don't look too happy at the prospect.'

She put her thoughts into careful chosen words, 'Well, I should feel rather isolated. I'd miss the company—the nurses and all the activity of a busy practice.'

She thought she had put that rather well but he said, 'Naturally, you'd have a nurse with you and the excitement of building up a rather run-down practice. It would be like setting up on your own, but with the advantage of being financially backed by me.'

'Yes, of course.' She knew she had lost the argument. 'Well, we'd better see what the practice is like. As you say, it's rather run-down. It might mean a lot of doing up and the expense might be too much.'

Rose had done her best, and as they had been talking she found that her mind was made up. She didn't want the job in spite of the inducements David kept bringing forward. She said, 'We shan't know anything until you've seen his books and the state of the surgery. Then there's the house. I suppose I'd have to live there.'

'No. Remember, the surgery is a separate building in the garden. You could stay in your present cottage and go backwards and forwards. It's only ten miles away.' He pointed to a signpost. 'Two miles—we're nearly there.'

Three hours later they drove back. At first they were silent, then with a quick glance at David, Rose said, 'Well, you've done it now. Are you pleased?'

David smiled. 'Yes. It's too good an opportunity to miss. Admittedly the old boy has been stuck in the past and we'll need lots of equipment, but we needn't get everything at once. I'll look in every day and be available if help is needed. As for the house—it needs doing up, of course, but I know a couple who would be willing to take it on at a low rental.' He paused, then asked, 'How do you feel about it?'

Rose kept her eyes on the road ahead and tried to keep her voice steady. 'Do you want my honest opinion?'

'Yes, of course.'

She waited while he drove past a big lorry, then she said slowly, 'I'm not sure. Always supposing that I stay working for you, it would mean all that you said—the excitement of building up a practice and so on. But—' She stopped.

'But? Go on.'

'Well, I'm not all that keen. I'm not terribly am-

bitious and I like my present job. I don't think I'd
be very happy there.'

He said nothing. Pulling in at a layby, he stopped
the engine and turned to look at her. Under his
searching gaze she flushed and said, 'I'm sorry, but
there it is.'

'The last thing I want is that you should be unhappy. You say you aren't ambitious—I'd no idea.
Don't you want eventually to have your own practice? Either as my partner in this branch or taking it
on as your own?'

She shifted uneasily in her seat. 'I really don't
know. It's very kind of you to give me this chance
but I'm very unsettled. I just don't know what I
want—I can't visualise my future.'

'Are you in love with somebody?'

The blunt question startled her and she stared at
him. For a moment she had a mad desire to tell him
that she loved him, but she bit her lip and shook her
head.

'Are you sure?' His voice was harsh. 'I wonder
if your indecision is due to Pete having, well, de-
serted you in favour of Anna?'

Oh, God, she thought resentfully, why does he
always harp back to Pete? How can I ever convince
him that he's got the wrong end of the stick? She
shook her head despairingly and spoke her thoughts
out loud. 'How can I convince you that Pete means
absolutely nothing to me?'

'I wish I could believe you but all the signs seem
to indicate the opposite. That's why—' He stopped
abruptly and she waited for him to continue, but he

shook his head and started the engine, pulling out into the road again. His face was grim and he said no more until they were well on their way. Then he said, 'Well, we had lunch with Mr Trent but how about having a drink to cheer ourselves up?'

'It would be nice,' she said, adding as he pulled up at the next pub, 'I'm sorry if I've disappointed you with regard to the branch practice. If you like, I'll give it a go for a while.'

'That's good of you but I can't bear the thought of you being unhappy. Let's leave it for a bit and see if we can arrange something else.'

They had nearly finished their drinks when his mobile phone rang. Taking it out of his jacket pocket, he listened for a moment then said, 'Right, I'll go there now.' In answer to the question in Rose's eyes he said, 'That was Wendy. Mr Roberts over at Down Farm wants me to see to a sow he's worried about. It's not far out of our way so we'd better go there now, instead of going back to the surgery first.'

Rose smiled to herself, wondering if Judith would be annoyed to see that David had his assistant vet with him again. It would be interesting to see her reaction.

CHAPTER EIGHT

As THEY drew near the Robertses' farm Rose said thoughtfully, 'I wonder if Judith will be there?'

'She may well be but she is between jobs and might have got one by now. I know she was expecting to get one very soon.' David paused, then added dryly, 'In any case, she won't be anywhere near the pigs.'

'Well, she says she has overcome her dislike of animals so she might be helping her father out.'

'Not necessarily.' David shot her a quick glance. 'You seem very interested in Judith and a bit cynical about her change of attitude towards animals. Don't you think it's genuine?'

That was an awkward question to answer so Rose merely shrugged and changed the conversation, wishing that she hadn't brought the subject up. To her relief, on arrival at the farm she was pleased to find that the only person with the pigs was Mr Roberts.

Indicating a large sow alone in a sty, he said, 'She farrowed yesterday but she won't let the piglets get to her. She obviously hasn't got any milk.'

'Soon put that right,' said David cheerfully, and took a syringe out of his case. 'All she needs is a dose of Pituitrin.'

'Mind how you go,' Mr Robinson warned. 'She

could turn nasty. If you like, I can get a plank and hold her in a corner.'

David shook his head. 'I don't think I'll need that. I'll be very quick.' So saying, he took the filled syringe and stepped into the sty. The sow, who was lying on her stomach, raised her head and grunted angrily, but before she could get to her feet David plunged the needle into the thin skin behind her ear. She heaved herself up and moved towards him menacingly, but David had retrieved the syringe and was out of the sty before she could attack him.

'Phew!' Mr Roberts wiped his forehead and David laughed.

'It works like a miracle—look.' He pointed at the piglets, who began to push one another to get at the milk, which began flowing copiously.

Mr Roberts heaved a sigh of relief. 'I've only just started keeping pigs but I'll know what's happening next time. Thank you.'

Invited in for a cup of tea, David—much to Rose's chagrin—accepted, and on the way to the house Mr Roberts said, 'Judy will be pleased to see you. She is going to London next week. She has got a job there but she will be coming down here for weekends.'

She came forward to greet them and was very effusive towards David but frowned at the sight of Rose. While her father talked about the sow, she came up to Rose and said in a whisper, 'Although I shall be working in London, I shall be back here at weekends so you needn't think you've seen the last of me.'

Rose gasped. 'What on earth do you mean?' She stared at the malicious look on the other girl's face.

'You know very well what I mean. I'm just warning you off David.' She turned away and joined in the general conversation, leaving Rose choking over her tea puce with anger. When the time came at last to leave, Judith, with a sly glance at Rose, went up to David and kissed him goodbye. It seemed to Rose that he visibly froze but, undeterred, Judith put her arms round him in an affectionate hug. His face was very red as he drew back and said goodbye to Mr Roberts who looked almost as embarrassed as David.

There was silence between David and Rose as they got in the car, but as soon as they were on the main road David said, 'What was Judith whispering to you about when Mr Roberts and I were talking? I caught a glimpse of your face and you looked furious.'

Rose hesitated. How could she tell him? It was too embarrassing. She said evasively, 'I can't remember. Something trivial, I'm sure.'

'Oh, come on Rose. You must remember. Why must you always be so secretive?'

His perceptive question hit home and she answered slowly, 'If you must know, she was warning me off.'

'Warning you off? What on earth do you mean? Warning you off what?'

Rose swallowed hard. 'You. Warning me off you. She said she would be here at weekends so I needn't think I'd seen the last of her. I didn't understand her at first but she then made it quite clear that she was warning me off you.'

'Good Lord!' She saw his whole body tense. 'What an insulting thing to say! The woman's mad!' He paused and glanced across at her. 'What did you say?'

'Nothing. I was stunned, and by the time I had recovered she had moved away.'

'What would you have liked to have said? Would you have said that she hadn't a hope?'

'No, of course not.' She could feel herself flushing, 'I think I would probably have said that she hadn't got anything to fear from me. I found it very humiliating, being cast in the role of rival.'

'Naturally.' His voice was dry. 'Well, forewarned is forearmed, as they say. I'd better see to it that I don't go over to the farm at weekends in future. I'll have to send Pete.'

'That's if Pete stays with us.'

'That's a point. I'll have to find a replacement for him.'

She said mischievously, 'I don't see why you should have to dodge Judith. You could go further and fare worse.' She knew she was needling him and began to regret her words when he subsided into silence. It lasted until they reached the surgery. Just before getting out, he gave her a long, searching look before he turned away.

Back inside, the nurses had nothing to report but David said, 'Let's have some tea. I've something to tell you all.' As soon as they were seated at the table he proceeded to tell them that he had bought Mr

Trent's practice and told them his plans for the future. When it came to the fact that he was hoping to put Rose in as branch manager, there was a collective gasp from his audience.

'Mind you,' he said with a quick glance at Rose, 'she hasn't yet made up her mind, but I'm hoping she will consider it favourably. We shall have to engage another veterinary nurse unless you—Wendy or Penny—would like to help run the new practice with her? You would have first chance.' He paused. 'Well, there it is—think it over. There's plenty of time. I don't suppose we shall move in for a couple of months.' He finished his tea and went into the office, leaving the nurses to turn their attention towards Rose.

She tried to answer their questions but wished they would stop asking her why she was hesitating about taking on the new branch practice. The more she thought about it the more she disliked the idea, but was unable to explain her reluctance. It was with relief that she heard the telephone ring and found herself talking to an agitated client whose collie had injured its leg and she thought it was broken. As she herself was unable to drive and had two small children, Rose told her that she would come and fetch the dog.

Susan said, 'I'm sorry, I can't go for you because I'm expecting a client soon to discuss the fate of a very old cat.' She paused. 'What will it be like with you over at the new practice? I'll be on my own then, won't I?'

Rose nodded. 'Yes, things will be different, but

you're quite capable of managing, you know.' She turned to the nurses. 'I must be off. Please will you get everything ready for our patient?'

Driving along, she reflected on Susan's lack of confidence and obvious fear of being in sole charge of the small animal section. They would probably need another vet as this present practice was increasing steadily. She sighed. What an upheaval it was going to be.

She really would prefer to stay in her present position and let David find someone else to run the branch practice. Perhaps she could persuade him to do that. Maybe he could put Susan in her place. As she drew near to the address she had been given, she put the plan to the back of her mind. She pulled up outside a small house where two young children ran out to greet her. Soon she was examining the collie, watched by its distressed owner.

Its front leg was indeed broken but, feeling it carefully, Rose said, 'I'll X-ray it, of course, but I think it is a clean break and simple to deal with.' Together they got the patient into her car and she drove off slowly and steadily. On arrival at the surgery she found everything ready for the operation. The X-ray confirmed her diagnosis and soon the dog was anaesthetised. Having set the leg into its proper position, she inserted a plate to secure it. As she was stitching up the wound David came in and stood silently watching. When the operation was over he came forward and lifted the dog from the table.

'I'll put him in the recovery cage,' he said, and she followed, thankful for his help. As she shut the cage door he turned to her. 'Come into the office, will you, please? I would really like to get something settled about the branch practice.'

She sighed and sat down opposite him, waiting for him to speak.

'I'm sorry to bring this up again so soon but when I first mentioned my idea you seemed quite keen. Now you give the impression that you have gone off the idea.' He paused. 'I know you say that you'll give it a go but that worries me. Won't you tell me honestly why you are so reluctant?'

She looked at him steadily. 'I've told you why. I'm not ambitious and I just don't fancy making such a change.' She went on, 'Why don't you offer it to Susan? I am sure she is quite capable now of working on her own.'

'Susan! Good Lord! You'd let her step over you? What's the matter with you, Rose? What has made you lose your ambition? There must be a reason— something personal?' He studied her searchingly— so intently that she looked away in confusion. He sighed. 'It must be to do with the possibility of Pete leaving. I can't think of anything else.'

She flushed angrily and got up from her chair. 'I've told you so many times that Pete means nothing to me but you simply won't believe me, will you?' She shook her head despairingly. 'I can see that I'll have to give up the idea of working here, much as I like it.'

He rose to his feet and came round the desk. He stood before her and said urgently, 'Don't do that, Rose, please. I can't do without you. I'll try to believe you about Pete. I really will.' He took a deep breath. 'Let's go back to where we were. You promised to give the branch a go. If you really hate it then come back here and I'll get someone else to run it.'

She weakened at the sight of his obvious distress and drew a calming breath. 'All right,' she said slowly, and took his outstretched hand. The feel of his strong grasp made her pulse race. She tried to withdraw but he held her firm for what seemed like eternity. Half hoping he would take her in his arms, she could feel her eyes burn with unshed tears, but at last he released her and she turned and went out of the room.

Avoiding the nurses, she went into the recovery room and stood by the cage, trying to concentrate her thoughts on the collie. He was coming round nicely after the operation and soon she was joined by Wendy.

'He'll be ready to go home tomorrow,' she said. 'Will you take him back after surgery?'

Rose nodded. 'That reminds me, I must give Mrs Harris a ring and tell her how he is.'

She went towards the telephone, but before she could pick it up Wendy said, 'About this branch practice. Penny and I have talked it over and agreed that if you decide to take it on I should like to go with you. That's if you would like me.' She paused. 'I suppose it means living in the house, but I won't mind.'

Rose looked at her gratefully. 'Thank you,

Wendy. I'd rather have you than anybody.' She turned suddenly. 'Here's David. Let's tell him.'

'I heard you.' He smiled at Wendy. 'That's good news. I'm sure you will help to make a success of it.' He went on, 'I've been thinking. There's no need for you to live in the house.' He turned to Rose. 'If you remember, the surgery itself is a separate building in the garden so when evening surgery is finished you can lock up and drive back here. The telephone can be put through here as well. As for the house, I can easily let that, knocking off a bit of the rent as compensation for having a surgery in the garden. What do you think about that?'

It certainly made the proposition more agreeable, and David was clearly pleased when she agreed. Later on Rose began to consider the implications. It seemed that David was determined to get her settled into the branch practice. Why, she wondered, was he so anxious? And why did she so dislike the idea of being separated from him during the day?

At last she had to admit to herself that it was because she was in love with him. But it was a hopeless case. She had hidden so much from him. He hated deceit and would, she felt sure, despise her if she ever opened up to him. If she ever found the courage to tell him everything, she doubted if he would ever forgive her or even understand.

A question burned on her mind. How did he feel about her? His statement that he wanted to marry her—was that genuine? It had been so strange and anyhow lately he seemed to have changed. All he was interested in was getting his branch practice going and using her to expand it.

She went to bed that night with no answer to her question and slept badly, only to be wakened in the early hours of the morning by the telephone. Half-asleep, she reached for the receiver and heard David's voice.

'I've just had a call from someone who's got a whelping bitch in difficulties. I asked them to bring it into the surgery, but they've got no means of transport so I said I'd go and fetch it. Will you get everything ready?'

Rose said quickly, 'Well, it's obviously a case for me so I'll go and get Wendy to help me.'

'No—there's no need for that. I don't want you to go out alone. And I'll be there to help if you have to operate.'

She realised he was determined so she said quietly, 'OK, have it your own way.' Hurriedly she put on some clothes and went over to the surgery, and half an hour later she heard David's car. He came in carrying a bundle in a blanket and put it on the table.

Turning to her, he said, 'She's in a bad way—been straining all day with no result. I think you'll have to do a Caesarean.'

Rose unwrapped the blankets and saw a very small mongrel, looking limp with exhaustion and nearly unconscious. She said, 'I'll give her an injection and see if that will start things moving.'

However, the poor animal was too worn out to

push any more so Rose shrugged hopelessly and said, 'It's no good, I'll have to operate.'

David nodded and filled a syringe. 'We'll get this into her and I'll look after the anaesthetic. Let's hope she survives.'

As soon as the bitch was unconscious Rose made the first incision and soon brought out an exceptionally large, dead puppy. 'This is what was holding things up,' she said. 'Let's hope the others will be smaller.' There were three other puppies, much smaller and all alive. They responded to a brisk rubbing by David, who placed them in the warm recovery cage, while Rose, having made sure there were no others, stitched up the incision. David handed her a syringe filled with Millophyline, a heart stimulant to help the mother come round quickly, then he carried the bitch and placed her gently into another cage.

As she washed her hands Rose said, 'Thank you for helping me. I'll wait here to make sure she comes round.'

'I'll wait with you,' he said calmly. 'I think we deserve a cup of tea.' He paused. 'You did a good job. Are you tired?'

She flushed with pleasure at his praise and looked at her watch. 'I'm wide awake now. It's five o'clock. Hardly worth going back to bed now.'

He said thoughtfully, 'A vet's life is a very demanding one. Do you ever regret having chosen it?'

'No,' she said firmly, then added slowly, 'But somehow I can't visualise growing old and still doing the same thing. Can you?'

'Yes. It's the life I've chosen and I wouldn't change it for anything.' He handed out two mugs of tea and sat down at the table where he drank deeply. Then he said, 'I expect your feeling about the future is a very natural urge for something more in your life. Marriage and children perhaps?' He looked at her searchingly. 'Have you any man in mind who you would like to give you those things?'

Confused, Rose took refuge in a long drink of tea, then, seeing that he was waiting for a reply, she said evasively with half a laugh, 'What a question!' She rose to her feet, saying, 'I'll have a look at our patient.' She went into the recovery room, where the little bitch was gradually coming round. As Rose stood, watching, her thoughts reverted to the conversation with David. If only he could read her mind.

What would his reaction be to the fact that she was in love with him? Hopelessly in love, she thought sadly. He seemed to have no wish to implement his former reckless pronouncement about wanting to marry her. It was probably only a game with him—a mild form of flirtation—though a rather peculiar one. He obviously did not want to take the opportunity of declaring himself again or even seizing the moment to kiss her. She sighed. He was indifferent towards her—there was no doubt about that.

The telephone rang suddenly, and automatically she reached for the receiver, noticing subconsciously that David was still sitting at the table deep in thought. Answering the call, she reassured the owner of the bitch that the operation was over and told her of the successful outcome. Rose added that the dog could be returned home next day. Turning after she'd hung up, she said to David, 'I think we can put the puppies in with their mother when she is fully conscious. It won't be long.'

'Just long enough to give us the opportunity for a serious talk,' he said. 'Finish your tea—it will get cold.'

She picked up the mug and drank deeply, then waited for him to begin. He seemed hesitant at first but suddenly he burst out, 'Rose, I wish I knew what goes on in your head. Are you intending to stay in my practice, either in your present job but as a partner or in charge of the branch practice? Or are you contemplating leaving me altogether and going to work for another vet?'

The direct questions put into words the very thoughts that had been worrying her constantly. She sat silently, looking down at her tea, until at last she lifted her head and met David's eyes steadily. The expression in them was so stern that she decided not to prevaricate and said, 'I honestly don't know about the first question, but as for the second one the answer is no. I'm not contemplating leaving and going to work for another vet.'

His eyes lit up. 'Well, thank God for that. As for the branch practice—I think you may well decide that you like being in sole charge and will build it up in no time.'

Suddenly she resented his calm assumption that

she would like being on her own and said sharply, 'You seem very anxious to get rid of me.'

'Get rid of you! Good heavens, Rose, what has put that idea into your head?'

'Well, it's obvious, isn't it? You could easily get someone else to take it on—why, even Richard might be glad of the chance, although he says he's already found somewhere, or you could advertise in the *Veterinary Record* or—'

He interrupted sharply. 'Yes, I could advertise, though I'm not keen, and I most certainly don't want Richard. I wanted to give you the chance.'

'Even though I don't want it?'

'That's what I can't understand,' he retorted. 'Anyone else would jump at the opportunity.'

'I've told you, I'm not ambitious,' she said resentfully, and saw his eyes grow cold. It was plain to her that he was thinking only of the practice and was not interested in her personal feelings. She got up from the table and said stiffly, 'You say you don't understand me but I don't understand you either.'

She paused, then said impulsively, 'Why don't you offer it to Pete?' Immediately she regretted her words but it was too late. She saw his face change as anger took over. Trying to explain, she added hastily, 'What I mean is he might not get a job with Anna's father and then he would jump at the chance.'

David said furiously, 'Pete, Pete—it always boils down to him, doesn't it? I think I do understand you after all. He's at the bottom of your lack of ambi-

tion—he's the one you're most concerned about.
Well, I can tell you straight. I won't have him as a
partner even if he doesn't leave of his own accord.
I've finished with him so you can stop pleading his
cause.'

She could have bitten her tongue off. Why, oh,
why had she spoken so foolishly? To her dismay
she felt her eyes fill and turned away hastily, but he
had seen and he took a step towards her.

'Rose—don't. I can't bear to see you cry. I'm
sorry—sorrier than you can ever know.' He stood
very close to her and she longed to throw herself
into his arms, but he hesitated and she realised that
she had done herself irrevocable damage. He held
out a handkerchief and she took it and wiped her
eyes furiously.

She said very quietly, 'I've made matters worse.
I'm not crying because—because—' She stopped.
'It's no use. You'll never understand.' She turned
and went out of the room, leaving him staring
after her.

CHAPTER NINE

FOR the next few days Rose avoided David as much as possible and he in turn seemed to keep his distance. Pete and Anna returned from their weekend away together, and the following day Anna told Rose that her father was willing to take Pete on as an assistant with a view to partnership and that she, Anna, would be leaving with him. Then she said, 'Pete has asked me to marry him, and when he has given a month's notice to David we're going to have a little party to celebrate our engagement.'

Rose congratulated her, trying not to show her doubts in view of Anna's glowing happiness. Anna smiled. 'Oh, I know you think I'm mad to take him on but we really love one another and I'm sure we'll be very happy together.'

It was when Pete came in to be congratulated that Rose began to think that, after all, he was a reformed character. He had given his notice to David that morning and said, 'I know I'm doing the right thing. My future lies with Anna's family's practice and with her help I'm sure we'll make a success of it.' He paused. 'We've had our differences, you and I, but can we let bygones be bygones?'

She took his hand and wished him well. From the corner of her eye she saw David, coming towards them. He glanced at her quickly, and as Pete and

Anna walked away there was a long silence until at last he said, 'Well, you've taken that very well, though it must be a bit of a blow to you.'

'Not at all,' she said coolly, adding, 'I think he and Anna will make a perfect couple. They seem very happy. What will you do now? Will you advertise for a replacement for Pete?'

He nodded thoughtfully. 'It may take some time to find the right man but I've had an idea. Would you like to do large animal work? Susan can manage on her own now and it would be useful experience for when you take on the branch practice. Although it will be predominantly small animals, you are bound to get queries for farm work or whatever. How about it?'

Surprised, she hesitated. It was an attractive idea and would certainly break the monotony. She knew she was capable of taking it on and it would be interesting experience. She saw he was waiting for her reply and at last she answered, 'I'd like that very much. Thank you.'

'Right. We'll start as soon as possible.' He smiled at her and her heart seemed to miss a beat. Then he turned and walked away and her spirits dropped at his businesslike attitude.

Still, she told herself, what could she expect? He obviously looked upon her purely as a colleague and maybe he thought he was consoling her for the loss of Pete. That's if he thought of her personal feelings at all.

The rest of the week passed uneventfully, and on Sunday Anna and Pete gave their engagement party.

It was, as Anna had said, only a small one as the main engagement party was being arranged at Anna's home. It was decided to hold it in the large sitting room in the nurses' house. They had all helped to prepare the food and had invited a few outside friends as well as all the veterinary staff.

Rose wore her prettiest dress and was rewarded with an admiring look from David who said, 'Good girl! You're putting a brave face on it.'

Infuriated, she took the drink he handed her and wished she dared throw it over him. After a while the floor was cleared for dancing. Suddenly David was at her side and pulled her into his arms. At first she was stiff and unyielding but he held her tight and gradually she relaxed.

He said softly, 'This is nice, isn't it?'

In a dream of love she nodded and smiled back at him. It was all too short, however, as Pete took the floor to make a speech, followed by David who congratulated the couple and wished them every happiness and proposed a toast.

After that there was more dancing and Rose found herself in great demand, so much so that there was no more time for another longed-for dance with David. Suddenly she saw him take his mobile phone out of his pocket and retreat into the next room in order to hear more clearly. He came back a few minutes later and went up to Pete and Anna.

Then he approached her and said, 'Just my luck! I must go over to Western Stables—a horse with colic.'

For Rose the magic of the evening had vanished so after a very short while she made her excuses and went home. It was becoming more and more evident to her that her happiness depended on being where David was. She sat, brooding over a cup of coffee and reflecting on her misfortune in loving a man who seemed now to look on her as merely a colleague. She wondered if she could carry on in such a situation.

How could she break down the barrier that seemed to have arisen? Would it be possible to tell him everything she had hitherto hidden from him? How, led by Pete, she had embarked on a trail of deceit. How— She shook her head violently. No. She wouldn't be able to bear his scorn. It would be too humiliating. The only way she could confess to him would be if she resigned from the practice, but she couldn't bear the thought of not seeing him again.

Getting up to wash up her cup, she was startled by the sound of the telephone. Picking it up, she listened to an agitated client. Could she come at once to see a dog who was choking on something caught in its throat? Looking at her watch, she saw it was ten minutes to midnight, and remembered David's rule that she should not go out at night to an unknown client. Accordingly, she asked the caller to bring the dog to the surgery. Reluctantly the man agreed. Putting down the receiver, she pulled on a jacket and went to open up the surgery.

While she was waiting she realised that she might need help, depending on the size of the dog. Wendy,

Penny and Susan were still at the party and it seemed a shame to call them away. She consoled herself with the thought that the dog's owner would be able to hold it while she did the examination. At last she heard the sound of a car and a few minutes later the door opened, but instead of the awaited client she was startled to see David who seemed as surprised as she was.

He said, 'What on earth are you doing? I left you at the party. I was just passing and saw the light.'

When he heard her explanation he said, 'Well, I'll stay here and give you a hand if it's needed.' He seated himself at the table and added, 'Why did you leave the party so early?'

She flushed. She couldn't tell him that when he had left everything had seemed completely flat. So she just murmured that she was rather tired.

He looked at her compassionately. 'And now you've got this emergency. Look, you go back and get to bed and I'll take this case over.'

His voice was very gentle and suddenly his kindness seemed almost too much to bear. To her horror she felt tears running down her cheeks. She knew it was too late to hide them from David.

'Rose!' He sounded aghast. 'What's wrong?' Reaching out, he took her by the shoulders and drew her to him. 'What have I said?'

She turned in his arms, but he held her tightly and for a few moments she let herself relax against him. Putting his hand under her chin, he bent his head to meet her lips, but at that moment they heard a car. He pulled out a handkerchief and wiped her eyes,

saying as he did so, 'Don't go home yet. I must
know why you are so sad.'

With an effort she pulled herself together and a
few minutes later a man came in with a small dog
in his arms.

'This is Tina,' he announced. 'See how she's
retching and clawing at her throat. She somehow got
hold of a chicken carcass and it's obvious that a
bone has got stuck in her throat.'

Placing the dog on the table, David held her while
Rose with difficulty opened the dog's mouth. There
was no need of an auroscope for the bone could be
plainly seen, lying across the back of the throat.
Forceps did the job and eventually produced half a
wishbone. When at last the grateful client had gone
there was a long silence, then David put the kettle
on.

Rose said, 'No, I don't want any tea, thank you.
I just want to get to bed.'

She went to pick up her jacket but David said, 'I
can't let you go, before finding out about your tears.
Please, Rose, won't you tell me what's wrong?'

Her heart was burning with love for him but all
she could say was, 'I've told you. I'm just tired.'

He looked at her long and searchingly then suddenly he said violently, 'I can guess, of course. It's
because of Pete and Anna's engagement. Oh, you
can shake your head but it's obvious.' He paused,
then his voice changed. No longer angry, he said
sympathetically, 'Can't you get him out of your
heart? Does he still mean so much to you? I hate to
think of you wasting your love on him. I know what

it's like—loving someone who treats you with indifference—but you just have to bear it and hope that eventually time will heal the wound.'

She stared at him incredulously. What did he mean? 'Someone who treats you with indifference.' To whom was he referring? Was he in love with someone who had let him down? He had turned away to see to the kettle. Over his shoulder he said, 'A quick cup of tea and then off to bed with you.'

'No, don't bother. I'll go now,' she said shakily, then added, 'Thank you for your sympathy but you've got it all wrong as usual.' She paused and impulsively said, 'Have you had an unhappy love affair?'

He turned quickly. 'I'm having it,' he said abruptly. Picking up the kettle, he resumed his tea-making. She went numb with shock, and when he came up to the table to hand her a mug of tea she avoided his eyes. His last words burned into her brain and her whole world seemed to fall apart. She longed to ask more, longed to know the details of his secret love, but most of all she needed to get away by herself to face up to this unwelcome shock she had suffered. Hurriedly she drank her tea then got up and washed up her mug. 'I'll go now,' she said. 'See you in the morning.'

He joined her at the door. 'Get in my car. I know it's only a few yards but it's quite chilly and very late.'

She was too tired to refuse and a few minutes later he pulled up at her cottage. He walked up the path with her, and as she unlocked her door he leaned forward and kissed her lightly on the cheek. 'Good-night,' he said. 'Don't cry any more. Pete's not worth it.'

A meaningless kiss, she thought bitterly as she got ready for bed and tried to face up to the fact that he was in love with somebody else. Trying to imagine who it could be, she gave up at last and closed her eyes.

Next morning David came into the surgery when they were having coffee. He joined in the talk about the party the previous night, seeming not to notice that Rose was listless and quiet. Then just as they finished he said, 'Rose, I have a horse to see which has gone lame. Would you like to come with me?'

She was immediately interested and asked a few pertinent questions.

He said, 'I'll come and pick you up after lunch— no, wait, I can do better than that. I'll come in about twelve-thirty and we can have a pub lunch together and go on to the horse from there. How does that sound?'

Rose thought quickly then nodded. There was nothing pending and Susan could cope on her own. When he had gone she continued her line of thought. It was true that Susan could manage on her own, and it suddenly struck her that her own position was becoming superfluous. Although the practice was very busy, there were times when she felt that the work she did could be done by a part-time vet.

Was that the reason David was so anxious for her to run the branch practice, rather than get rid of her? Suddenly worried, she decided to ask him, though

whether he would answer was debatable. He was so
secretive. She never knew how his mind was working and now that he had told her he was suffering
from a hopeless love affair she realised that she
never really understood him. But he in his turn had
never understood her. They were both, it seemed, at
cross purposes.

Suddenly, like a flash, an idea came into her
mind. Why not, she asked herself, confess the reason
she had deceived him and rid herself of the burden
of guilt she felt whenever he questioned her? After
all, she had nothing to lose. The difficult would be
in making him listen and stop jumping to conclusions. Turning the idea over, she wondered if this
pub lunch would be a good opportunity. Nervously
she rejected it. It might be better to make a proper
appointment to see him. But then they might well
be interrupted by an urgent call.

The truth was, she admitted to herself, she was
frightened, feeling that she knew how he would re-
act to her deception. She sighed and tried to pull
herself together. She must wait for the right moment
and try to make him listen and understand.

CHAPTER TEN

DAVID was silent as they drove out to the country. When at last he began to talk he made no mention of the party the night before. Instead he spoke professionally about the treatment he was going to give the horse at the stables.

'I saw him yesterday,' he said, 'and he is in a certain amount of pain from arthritis. I'm going to give him some more phenylbutazone which, as you know, is a wonder drug for horses. He'll be OK in a few days.' He paused. 'Soon it will be banned.'

Rose was surprised. 'What do you mean? Why on earth should it be banned? By what authority?'

'Oh, haven't you heard? It's in one of the veterinary journals and it's a piece of future EU registration. Just because in certain European countries horses and ponies are food-producing animals, it is maintained that there is a risk of medicinal residue being passed on to humans.' He paused and there was anger in his next words. 'It's nonsense, of course. It's been used successfully in the treatment of pain in horses for over forty years and for many years in human medicine also. I've taken it myself when I've sprained my back, and in a matter of three days it has completely cleared up the trouble.

'Now, with this new regulation banning it in the horsemeat food industry, it will probably become economically not worthwhile for the manufacturers to produce and many horses and ponies will suffer needless pain when phenylbutazone is no longer available. Alternative drugs are offered but they are less effective.' He then went on indignantly, 'Legislation in the EU is supposed to respect the rights of animals to enjoy health and welfare but this is just a direct denial of this directive. How can we vets continue with our legal responsibilities to our patients?'

Rose shared his indignation and was so interested that she forgot her personal worry. It was not until she was seated in a pretty country pub that, with a sinking heart, she realised that here was the perfect opportunity she had been waiting for to try and make her confession of guilt.

Drawing a long breath, she pushed aside her salad and said, 'David, I want to tell you something you are not going to like.' She hesitated for a moment.

He took her up hastily. 'Don't tell me. I can guess. You are going to say you really don't want to run the branch practice. Well, if that's so I won't force you. I'll look out for someone else.' He paused and looked at her closely. 'You shake your head. Does that mean something more serious? Don't tell me you are going to leave the practice altogether?' He reached across the table and took her hand. 'What's brought this on?'

She tried to withdraw her hand but he held it more tightly and suddenly her courage failed. She said tremulously, 'It's not what you think at all, but I can see this isn't the right moment.' She glanced at her watch. 'It will take too long and there's this horse to be seen.'

'Now you're tormenting me.' He let go of her hand. 'I'll never understand you, Rose. What are you hiding from me?' He looked at her so pleadingly that her resolution failed. How could she destroy his trust in her by telling him her sordid little story of deception—deception from the very beginning of their acquaintance?

She drew a long breath and said tentatively, 'You're right. I am hiding something from you but…' she looked around the crowded pub '…there are too many people here. I'll have to choose a better moment.'

He frowned, took up his glass and had a long drink. Then he said coldly, 'Well, I suggest you come to my house when we've finished with the horse. We'll have an hour or two before evening surgery.'

She tried to speak lightly. 'Always supposing there are no more calls for either of us.'

'Of course. Now finish your salad and we'll be going.'

It was difficult to eat under his searching gaze, but at last she pushed her plate away and said, 'I'm not very hungry. Let's go.'

She could feel David's displeasure as he drove along, and her apprehension grew. How would he receive her confession? Most likely with cold contempt in view of his almost pathological hatred of deceit. How could she bear his scorn? Suddenly she wondered if it would be better not to tell him at all.

Get out of it somehow and let things go on as they were at present. But she had already said too much and he would be furious if she told him she had had second thoughts about opening up to him. Well, she must hope he would listen to her and not cut her short with his own conclusions, as he always seemed to do.

Absorbed in her thoughts, she was surprised when he said, 'We're here.'

Hastily she pulled herself together as they drove into the yard. Here she was introduced to the head groom, who led them to one of a row of loose boxes and said, 'He's better already. That stuff you gave him certainly works like magic.'

When he was led out into the yard the magnificent animal stood quietly while David examined him. He stood back and said, 'He'll be OK in a couple of days. But what's going to happen when this new EU regulation becomes law I really don't know.'

The groom nodded. 'You told me about it yesterday. But surely it won't affect us here, will it? When we lose a horse we don't sell it for horsemeat.'

David shrugged. 'You'll have to prove it and, what's more, the demand for phenylbutazone will become less and most probably the manufacturers won't find it profitable to produce.'

'Well, let's be optimistic,' said the groom. 'One thing I know is that none of our animals are going to be turned into horsemeat for a lot of continental butchers.'

As they drove away David said, 'Well, I won't say I share his optimism. In fact, I'm in a very pessimistic mood today and your threat of something unpleasant to tell me is the last straw.'

Rose made no reply, and after a quick glance at her David said no more until they reached the surgery. Then he said, 'We'd better look in here first, then we'll go to my house.'

The nurses welcomed them back with obvious relief. Wendy said, 'I was just going to ring you on your mobile. There's a message for you, David. It's from the vet whose practice you are going to buy. He wants you to ring him back as soon as possible.'

'I'll ring him from the office,' David said, and left Rose undecided as to what to do next. Wendy asked about the horse and that provided conversation until David came back into the room.

'He wants some changes in the contract. Honestly, the old boy quibbles about everything.' He turned to Rose and said, 'I have to go and see him to straighten things out. We'll have to change our plans.' He paused. 'I tell you what—let me take you out to dinner tonight. Don't shake your head. I'll pick you up after surgery, say about eight o'clock. Would you be able to book a table for us at the Red House?'

It was no use protesting in view of the curiosity on the faces of the others so Rose went to telephone the hotel. Then she had to make some kind of explanation to the nurses, which she did by saying that she and David were going to discuss the terms of her appointment at the branch practice. That seemed to satisfy them. But the thought of sitting over a dinner table to tell David the sad tale of her deceit made her heart sink.

She had no urgent work to do so she decided to go back to her house and look for something suitable to wear for the evening. Her apprehension grew as she looked through her clothes but eventually, having made her choice, she put everything in readiness and made up her mind to leave evening surgery in plenty of time. Then, over a cup of tea, she tried to assemble her thoughts. She would have to begin at the very beginning and try and explain how she had had to prevaricate on various occasions in order not to betray Pete. If only David would hear her out and not flare up at the first mention of Pete's name.

Perhaps after all it was just as well that her confession was to be made in a public place. David would have to hold onto his temper and she would have to keep her emotions in control. Gradually her spirits rose. There was nothing very terrible to confess—most of the time her deception had been the result of David's fixation that she was in love with Pete. All the same, it was not going to be easy in view of David's obsession for honesty and trust. It would be devastating if he turned against her, but she needed to rid herself of the burden of guilt that had built up and was weighing her down. Her conscience would then be clear.

One thing puzzled her and that was David's declaration that he intended to marry her. Had that just been a bad joke? He had never referred to it again and now he said he was suffering from an unhappy love affair. Perhaps this evening he might open up and tell her about it.

That evening, Rose gave a final look at herself in the mirror when she heard David's car. When she opened her front door he came in and gave her an admiring look.

'You look very glamorous. That blue dress—it really emphasises your beautiful eyes.'

She flushed and, rather confused, she said, 'There's plenty of time. Would you like a coffee?'

'Good idea,' he said, and followed her into the kitchen. 'I'll make it,' he said, and in spite of her protests he set to and in a few minutes he put two steaming mugs on the table. Sitting opposite him, she could find nothing to say at first, then finally decided to ask him about his visit to the old vet.

He gave an exasperated groan. 'He wants to put off the date of my taking over. I've had to agree but it'll mean a delay of a couple of months. I only hope he doesn't back out altogether.'

'Oh, dear! Do you think that's likely?'

'Not really. I think he needs extra time to get into the cottage he's bought down in the West Country. It's just that I'm so anxious to take over the practice that I get nervous.'

She laughed. 'You, nervous! That's not like you.'

He looked at her over the rim of his coffee-mug. 'You don't know me very well, then. I get worked up inside. Just as I am now at the thought of what you might be wanting to say to me. Can you give me a clue as to what it's all about?'

She swallowed her coffee hurriedly and choked.

After she had recovered she shook her head. 'I'd rather not. You might not want to take me out to dinner.'

'Oh, dear! But nothing would make me treat you like that.' He glanced at his watch, 'We'd better be going.'

Seated in his car, Rose wondered when she should begin to tell him and tried to rehearse an opening sentence. Finally she decided to wait until the coffee stage.

The restaurant was full but their table was secluded, and once they were seated they were handed two large menus to study. David made his choice very quickly and sat watching Rose as she tried to decide. Her appetite had completely disappeared and she sighed at the vast choice.

'Let me help you.' He took the menu from her. 'They have a very good chef here.'

Momentarily she wondered if he had taken another girl to this place, and asked impulsively, 'Are you in the habit of coming here?'

'I usually bring my mother here when she occasionally comes to visit me.'

Rose waited while he dealt with the wine waiter, then she said, 'Is your mother still practising?'

'Yes, though I believe she is thinking of giving up soon.'

'How do you feel about that?' Rose asked, putting off her own problem in favour of learning more about the man she loved.

He looked at her thoughtfully. 'Well, it doesn't affect me much. I wasn't close to my parents. I suppose I think of it as a tragedy for my father and complete selfishness on the part of my mother.'

'You feel that she should have sacrificed her career in order to please your father?'

'That's a harsh way of looking at it.' His voice was grim. 'I suppose it comes down to that, doesn't it?' He frowned. 'I can only conclude that she didn't really love him.' He stopped and picked up his glass and drank deeply. Then he added, 'The strange thing is that she was always on at me to get married.'

Rose said thoughtfully, 'Why were they unable to work together in the same practice?'

He shrugged. 'That's what always puzzled me, but I now think it was professional rivalry. They were both very strong-willed and would disagree on almost everything.'

'So that's why you have such a thing about married vets in the same practice?' Rose saw the conversation leading her on to what she had to say but still she hesitated to take the plunge.

'Yes,' he said briefly, then added slowly, 'I may be wrong, but my experience of being shovelled off to boarding school and feeling that I was always in the way has left me convinced that a mother's place is with her children.'

Rose concentrated on dissecting the Dover sole on her plate. As she lifted off the backbone she said, 'I don't know what the statistics are of married couples working happily together, in spite of having children, but I am sure your parents were in the minority.' Seizing the opening, she drew a long breath and continued, 'Well, what you have told me leads

me on to what I have to tell you.' She paused and
saw him stiffen. She went on reluctantly. 'I feel I
have deceived you in many ways. I have to go back
to the beginning when I first came here. It began
with Pete—'

He interrupted fiercely. 'Ah, Pete! I might have
known he would be the cause of any trouble.'

She shook her head. 'I was as much to blame as
he was.' She proceeded to tell the whole story of
how she had broken off their engagement, then how
she had reacted when she had found out from Pete
how David felt about married vets working together
in the same practice, maintaining that as she and
Pete were no longer engaged that objection would
not apply. From then on her tale was of evasion and
deceit in many ways, and how difficult it had been
to shake off Pete and how impossible it had been
to convince David that she had never been in love with
Pete.

'I hated hiding things from you but I was caught
in a web, and although I tried to convince you that
Pete meant nothing to me you always got the wrong
end of the stick.'

Stealing a quick glance at him, her heart sank.
His face was frozen and his eyes hard. She waited
for his reaction nervously. For a few minutes, which
seemed an eternity, he sat in silence. Unable to bear
it, she said tremulously, 'So now you know and I
expect you hate me.'

'Don't!' He was breathing fast. 'Please, don't
blame yourself so bitterly. I realise now that it is all
my fault. What a fool I've been. So wrapped up in

my preconceived ideas. Laying down the law and refusing to see any other point of view.' He paused. 'I need time to readjust my mind but right now all I can do is to ask you to forgive me.'

To her dismay she could feel tears running down her cheeks, and hastily she searched for a handkerchief. Silently he passed her one, and as she took it he put his other hand out and grasped hers.

'You'll have to stop—' his voice cracked '—or you'll have me joining you. I can't bear to see you cry.' He waited while she wiped her eyes. Still holding her hand, he added, 'There is so much I want to say to you but this is neither the time nor the place. Let's finish this delicious meal.'

She let her hand remain in his, then suddenly recalled his comment about being in the middle of a hopeless love affair. She said, 'Let's talk about something else—you, for instance. Why did you say the other day that you were suffering from a hopeless love affair?'

'Ah!' She felt his hand tighten on hers. 'That is something that needs sorting out.'

She felt a chill run right through her and, gently withdrawing her hand, she tried to concentrate on the remainder of her meal. At last she broke the silence. 'It's very good of you to blame yourself but the fact remains I wasn't completely honest with you. I don't suppose you will ever quite trust me again.'

He looked up and she saw a muscle twitch at the side of his face. 'I would trust you with my life,' he said quietly, and once more reached for her hand. Her heart leapt for a moment, then disbelievingly she told herself that he was just thinking of her as a friend.

Suddenly he said, 'I want to tell you something but when I think of all my foolish dogmatic statements I hardly dare.' He paused and his eyes seemed to hold hers with an intensity that made her tremble and look away. He said very quietly, 'I can't hold it back. I love you, Rose. I've loved you from the first moment we met but I was so sure that you loved Pete that I considered my love doomed.' He paused and waited but she made no reply. Her heart was so full that her throat was choking. 'Rose…' His voice was pleading. 'How do you feel about me? Have I got a chance?'

'What about your hopeless love?' She asked the question, although she felt she knew the answer.

'Rose,' he said reproachfully, 'don't torment me. You are the only girl I have ever loved or ever will. I thought it was hopeless because you seemed so indifferent to me. Rose…' His voice trembled. 'Please.'

She sat in silence for a long moment then she said softly, 'I can't believe what I'm hearing. Do you really mean that there is no one else?'

'Of course there isn't. We seem to have misunderstood one another from the start.'

As their eyes met she saw such deep tenderness that her heart seemed to melt inside her. Her eyes fell before his beseeching gaze and she nodded mutely.

'Oh, my darling!' His grasp on her hand tightened. Looking around, he said quickly, 'Let's get out of here.'

Rose sat in a daze while he settled the bill and then he led her out into the garden where they walked until they were out of sight of anyone. Silently he took her in his arms and before they kissed he said, 'Say it, Rose, please—say you love me.'

She could hear the passion in his voice and all her being responded. 'Yes, darling David, I love you with all my heart.'

Then he kissed her and all the past misunderstandings melted away as they clung to one another. Later, much later, as they drove back he said, 'We won't make the mistakes my parents made. We'll work together and share the practice. That is, if you have no objection.'

She laughed gently. 'That depends on how many children we have.'

He shot her a quick glance and smiled. 'That will depend on you, my darling.'

She sighed happily as she visualised the future— a home filled with love and laughter and mutual interests. There would be no need for secrecy and she would make up to him for his lonely childhood.

The rest of the evening passed in a daze of anticipation for Rose. David, too, seemed in seventh heaven and kept stealing glances at her as though to reassure himself that she was real. When at last they reluctantly parted he said softly, 'Let's keep our secret to ourselves for a while, shall we?'

Rose nodded. There was plenty of time to share the fact of their love with others. It was a love that was almost too precious to be exposed to comments and congratulations.

Next morning when Rose went into the surgery she hoped fervently that her joyful face would not betray her, but she need not have worried for to her astonishment she found Richard there. He was deep in conversation with Penny and Wendy, and Penny in particular looked embarrassed as he broke off and turned to Rose.

'I've come early to see if I can catch David. I'd like to have a word with him.' He paused. 'Ah, I think that's him.' He turned as the door opened and said to David as he entered, 'Can you spare me a few moments, please? I have a proposition to put to you.'

David nodded and as the office door closed behind them Penny said, 'What a charmer! I could go for him in a big way.'

Rose laughed. 'Well, as far as I know, he's available so you can get to work on him.' She went on, 'I wonder what he wants with David.'

She was soon to know because a few minutes later the door opened suddenly and David called her to join them. Pulling out a chair for her, he said, 'I'd like your opinion on an idea that Richard has put to me. Apparently, he can't get planning permission for the place he wanted.' He turned to Richard. 'Tell her yourself. As my future partner she will be involved.'

Richard hesitated for a moment. Turning to Rose,

he said, 'Well, after the failure with that place I contacted Mr Trent, but he told me he had already sold his practice to David. So that seemed to be that, but then an idea came to me and this is what it is. Could you take me on as your assistant and let me run the branch practice for you?'

Rose was so startled that she was speechless. It seemed a very good idea but she didn't want to appear to be encouraging Richard. She looked appealingly at David but his face was expressionless. At last she said, 'Well, I'm not a partner yet so I'm going to leave it to David to decide.' She paused. 'I think we had better have a little time to think it over, don't you?'

Richard looked disappointed but David's face cleared and he nodded. 'Yes,' he said firmly. 'We'll talk it over and let you know tomorrow.'

With that Richard had to be content. David accompanied him to the door. On his way out Richard smiled at Penny who gave him a beaming smile in return. Rose stayed in the office and waited for David's return. When he came back he shut the door behind him, put his arms round her and said slowly, 'I have only one objection. I wonder if you can guess what it is.'

Looking up at him, she said frankly, 'You don't like the idea of him being in the same practice as I am.'

He nodded slowly. 'Well, I think it is a dangerous situation. He's very keen on you and it seems like asking for trouble.'

She sighed. 'You don't trust me, do you?'

'Of course I trust you. It's him I don't trust.' His face was so troubled that Rose's heart sank.

She said quietly, 'David, I love you deeply—more perhaps than you'll ever know. But you evidently don't really trust the depth of my love. You think I could be enticed away by someone else. How can I convince you that you're wrong?'

She was near to tears and suddenly his arms tightened around her. His voice was broken as he bent to kiss her.

'My darling, you're absolutely right. I find it hard to believe that you really love me and I'm terrified that you might find that you've made a mistake.'

She reached up and stroked his hair. His loveless childhood had left its scars and it would be her life's work to heal them. She said, 'Let Richard come. He means nothing to me. He's got over me already— did you see how interested he was in Penny and she in him?' She paused as he held her even tighter. 'Let's tell everyone now that we are engaged and let's get married as soon as possible. Then you will see how much I love you and always will do.'

He crushed her to him and gave a great sigh of joy as their lips met in a kiss that seemed to last for ever.

MILLS & BOON®

Makes any time special

Enjoy a romantic novel from
Mills & Boon®

Presents...™   *Enchanted*™   TEMPTATION.

Historical Romance™   √MEDICAL
ROMANCE®

SANDRA BROWN

TIGER PRINCE

**Caren was in need of a holiday away
from her high pressured Washington D.C.
job. Derek was trying to escape the
scandal-hungry press. They both found
the perfect hideaway, and shared blissful
days in Jamaica, and only half truths.**

**But then Caren learned the price she
would have to pay...**

4 FREE

books and a surprise gift!

We would like to take this opportunity to thank you for reading this Mills & Boon® book by offering you the chance to take FOUR more specially selected titles from the Medical Romance™ series absolutely FREE! We're also making this offer to introduce you to the benefits of the Reader Service™—

- ★ FREE home delivery
- ★ FREE gifts and competitions
- ★ FREE monthly Newsletter
- ★ Exclusive Reader Service discounts
- ★ Books available before they're in the shops

Accepting these FREE books and gift places you under no obligation to buy, you may cancel at any time, even after receiving your free shipment. Simply complete your details below and return the entire page to the address below. *You don't even need a stamp!*

YES! Please send me 4 free Medical Romance books and a surprise gift. I understand that unless you hear from me, I will receive 6 superb new titles every month for just £2.40 each, postage and packing free. I am under no obligation to purchase any books and may cancel my subscription at any time. The free books and gift will be mine to keep in any case.

M0EA

Ms/Mrs/Miss/Mr ....Initials...................................
BLOCK CAPITALS PLEASE

Surname ....

Address ....

....

....Postcode...............................

Send this whole page to:
UK: FREEPOST CN81, Croydon, CR9 3WZ
EIRE: PO Box 4546, Kilcock, County Kildare (stamp required)

MARY LYNN BAXTER

ONE SUMMER EVENING

she could never forget...

Cassie has been living a nightmare since she left her parents' luxurious home nine years ago after a reckless act of love changed her life forever. Now she believes she's safe and has returned... but danger has followed her.

Published 21st January 2000

Available from all good paperback stockists.

MIRA®